About the Author

Chris is a former solicitor and part-time judge. He lives with his wife in East Anglia. A qualified pilot and supporter of England Rugby. Along with writing, he enjoys travelling and photography.

Stella

Chris Orr

Stella

Olympia Publishers
London

www.olympiapublishers.com
OLYMPIA PAPERBACK EDITION

Copyright © Chris Orr 2023

The right of Chris Orr to be identified as author of
this work has been asserted in accordance with sections 77 and 78 of
the Copyright, Designs and Patents Act 1988.

All Rights Reserved

No reproduction, copy or transmission of this publication
may be made without written permission.
No paragraph of this publication may be reproduced,
copied or transmitted save with the written permission of the publisher,
or in accordance with the provisions
of the Copyright Act 1956 (as amended).

Any person who commits any unauthorised act in relation to
this publication may be liable to criminal
prosecution and civil claims for damage.

A CIP catalogue record for this title is
available from the British Library.

ISBN: 978-1-80074-840-8

This is a work of fiction.
Names, characters, places and incidents originate from the writer's
imagination. Any resemblance to actual persons, living or dead, is
purely coincidental.

First Published in 2023

Olympia Publishers
Tallis House
2 Tallis Street
London
EC4Y 0AB

Printed in Great Britain

Dedication

This book is dedicated to my mother and my late father.

Acknowledgements

My grateful thanks go to my dear wife for all her support and patience with me during this journey. Also, to my editor for the tireless work she put in with me, thanks Heather. Finally, those of you who read the drafts and told me to keep going, I hope you like the final product.

Chapter 1

Stella sat nervously on the bench, shoulders hunched, head bowed and looking at her hands. They were clasped tight and resting on her lap. The bench was made of cold steel and painted red; graffiti scratches declaring love and hate were etched between individual names and nicknames. How the hell had it come to this? The corridor had several such benches, all the same, occupied by a variety of individuals, mostly with short hair, tattoos and clothes from Primark. Walls, standard magnolia looking tired. A couple of vending machines and a water cooler were the sole source of sustenance. There were doors marked as toilets that, frankly, Stella had no desire to investigate any further. Also, the corridor held a number of other rooms with keypad locks and no suggestion as to what is behind them, save for chicken wire viewing windows inset. The booking-in area was run by people in black gowns behind glass. They had a distinct lack of enthusiasm about them. As for the 'Primark Posse,' trainers, T-shirts, and the aroma of stale cigarettes (or something more herbal) was flavour of the day. Elasticated grey tracksuit bottoms, which customarily failed to cover the top of their arse and thus exposed, as a symbol of fraternity, the brand of underwear for all. Many in their twenties except for some elderly, homeless looking people, and the smell of body odour was intense, making Stella want to retch.

Alongside these were a curious bunch of suits, various shapes, genders and mostly in their fifties looking less than enthusiastic about the day. A couple of others stood out, more people wearing gowns, or was it the same ones that booked Stella in, she had no idea. The gowns were torn, unpressed and ill-fitting. Beneath the gowns men wore shirts with ties, top buttons open and the women tired looking blouses. Nothing matching, but the gowns created a functional distinction from the other suits. Had Stella overdressed? She felt seriously out of place. Inch heels, navy skirt hemline touching the top of the knee, crisp white blouse and a jacket. She had applied only a little make-up and her hair hung down to her shoulders, as it had for the last twenty years. Her nails, freshly manicured and painted. She was the best dressed person there.

A crushed-gown gent (Dave, according to his badge) had taken her name when she booked in and asked if she needed help. She said that she didn't and was handed a form to complete. It was a list of all her income, meagre compared to this time last year, and outgoings. She took the form and completed it with her classic Parker, which she always carried in her bag. She sat and waited, her nervousness causing random biting of her cheek. Meanwhile, the suits walked the corridor calling names and taking the owners of the names to various side rooms, or stood having a discussion in the corridor, which was getting more crowded. The odd suit had a chat with another suit, at times congenial and at times serious, judging by the facial expressions. One thing was clear though, all were going through the motions of the day.

The gowns started calling names and taking the Primark posse into various rooms.

"Give em hell mate. Don't take no shit bro."

"Fuck 'em, I won't. Jumped up bastards."

Sometimes suits would also go in, following behind. Most of the

Primark posse exited with suits, a shake of hands ended the interaction between them.

"Well done, you fucking told them," and to the crowd, "showed them tossers what's what."

Randomly, it seemed a suit would come out alone with a dejected look on their face, a subdued shake of the head to the crowd who bowed their heads and mimicked the head shake.

Stella sat for what seemed like an age, time seemingly stopped, while suits, gowns and posse continued in an unending flow in an out of rooms. Smells and bad language abounding and flowing through the corridor, an invisible vapour haze of poverty. She watched nervously waiting to be assaulted – or worse – trying to keep her head down and to disappear into the bench like a chameleon, not wanting to be seen, not wanting to even be there.

A gown, not Dave, exited a door and called her name, "Stella Green?" She rose from the bench and without warning, her legs turned to jelly and Stella began to shake. Was this it? Were these the final steps when her life could go no lower? She had told no one. Would her friends and neighbours even miss her? How long before they noticed? What would they say? Oh, the shame. She walked slowly, eyes staring with tunnel vision at the doorway ahead, her mind having to concentrate on the simple task of moving her legs, following the gown through the door, a small inner lobby and another door.

The room was bright, three rows of bench seating, cushioned this time but worn, a glass half screen and more cinema seats. Then she noticed the people. One suit, his back to her facing another. At the back another single suit sitting above the rest, looking down, watching and waiting, behind him a crest on the wall. The gown (Alan, it transpires from his badge) led her to a box, a glass fronted box with a locked door, wooden bench inside and a large metal rear door. The glass was full ceiling height.

"In here please and face the clerk."

Stella complied. The clerk, a pleasant looking lady in her early thirties, mousy brown hair and a smile said, "Are you Stella Green?"

Stella confirmed her name with a shaky voice and a tear started to roll down her cheek.

Peter Snowdon, the Judge, looked on unmoved. He had seen these crocodile tears many times before and was not to be taken in by such third-rate, drama-student antics. Stella confirmed her age and nationality. When asked her address she said, "Oh my, must I? What if I am in the papers, my neighbours, my friends, I don't want to go to prison." With that her legs gave way and she collapsed in a heap on the floor, unable to control a river of tears running down her cheeks and creating small, distinct pools on the floor.

Judge Snowdon had rarely seen such an Oscar-winning collapse, but he was not falling for it. "Come on, get on with it, what's your address?" Loud and in an authoritarian manner, despite this he was not a bully.

"Sir," the gown said, "I think Miss Green could do with a moment to compose herself. Perhaps, sir could put the case back and Miss Green might speak with Mr Hughes? We have other matters ready."

"Very well, Miss Green, go back outside and speak with Mr Hughes. I will see you later." Snowdon was not impressed at this acting, what was wrong with her? He had seen her record. She didn't look like a regular but had been in court several times; this was not her first drink drive matter.

Alan helped her up and took her outside. "Wait here, Mr

Hughes will find you soon."

In the corridor once more, this time the posse looked on quizzically. She overheard a few of them say, "What had happened? The bitch will have put Snowdon in a bad mood now that's for sure. We are for it, shit!"

The Posse gave her a few Paddington bear stares, not that she noticed, head in hands trying to stem the tears, compose herself, and stop herself from running out of the building, to be anywhere but here. A few moments later a suit came up to her, mid-fifties, well dressed but tired looking.

"Stella Green?" She lifted her head and nodded. "I am David Hughes, the duty solicitor. Give me ten minutes to get your papers emailed and we can have a private chat." Stella nodded again, and then returned her gaze to her shoes and the floor in between them.

David Hughes was a solicitor. He was fifty-seven years old and had been divorced without children for a decade or more, he forgets how quickly time passes. For over thirty years he had been a criminal defence lawyer. It was his devotion to his work that killed his marriage. During the working day he was in court or in police stations. In the evening he worked on the next day's cases, if he had the time or energy, or in the police station. In his thirty-odd years he had built up a loyal group of clients, and was busy. Respected by the courts, he got good deals and outcomes for those he represented in the main. It was the pressure of work that led to his failed marriage and lack of children. Yes, he missed her and yes, he would have loved a child, a legacy to continue his work. He had been a firm believer in fighting for the rights of the underdog, the defendant who, in law, was innocent until proved guilty. The might of the state and years of cutbacks across the whole justice system had changed all that, now it was merely a way to pay the mortgage and the bills. No, he could not afford to retire, or he would have done so five years earlier. Now retirement was a pipe dream, and apathy for the cause was beginning to set in.

It was more than the promised ten minutes, but eventually David Hughes appeared at Stella's side, "Miss Green?"

Stella nodded again, looking up once more at the person who would save her from the endless downward spiral and revive her life to a level where she could once again be proud of herself.

"Come with me, let's get a private room."

She complied, still mute, and followed David down the hallway. She watched him as he entered a combination and unlocked the door. Inside the room, a simple office desk with four chairs, all mismatched. David sat one side and beckoned Stella to sit opposite.

"Miss Green, just to remind you, I am David Hughes, I am the duty solicitor and my cost to you today is picked up by the state. For what it's worth, I'm here to give you advice, to explain the procedure and, if necessary, to speak for you in court. I am not here to give you defences or tell you what happened as I wasn't there. I know you have been through the system several times already and probably know all of that already, but I make a point of telling everyone I meet for the first time. Just to be sure they and you understand."

Been through the system, several times! What was he saying? "Mr Hughes—"

"You can call me David, everyone does."

"Ok David, I really don't understand what you are saying, I have never been in a criminal court in my life."

David looked puzzled and opened up his iPad. He pressed a few buttons on the attached keyboard, swiped here, more buttons and yet more swiping. "Miss Green—"

"If you are David, I am Stella."

"Ok, Stella, I'm now confused. Let me run through a few things with you, if I may?" He checked name and date of birth, no problem, even place of birth checked out. "You are here for driving with excess alcohol, no?"

"Yes," she replied. "Ninety-five in breath they said. It's a terrible mistake, I had a bad night, drank too much, and felt sorry for myself 'til about three, ate nothing and was on my way to yoga at seven thirty when I got stopped for missing a give-way they said."

It was all checking out so far, Stella was confirming what David knew, and more.

"Right then. Now, when I look at your previous convictions everything checks out except, that they have an old address in Newmarket for you. You were last convicted two years ago for shop theft, a couple of minor other matters going back a bit and crucially, a drink drive conviction seven years ago. I must say, you don't look like the kind of person with this history."

"That's because I'm not. I've lived at the same house in Thurston for at least the last fifteen years, and I have never been in trouble with the law before."

David mused for a moment, his left eye partially closed and forehead slightly furrowed, he had not seen this for some time. There were many would have struggled to work out how this could be, preferring simply to quietly and in their own heads disbelieve the client. After all, these are the criminal fraternity we are dealing with, not known for their honesty in most matters. Normally you only had to explain to them why their version simply did not stack up and once you got that far, you could bring them back to a reality. This time David was before a smartly-dressed lady, clearly upset and confused, way out of her depth, and the Police National Computer record of her convictions did not fit the client. He believed she was the victim of identity theft.

"Ok Stella, this is important. This list of previous convictions shows a drink drive within the last ten years, so there is a minimum ban of three years, probably four given the reading. Also, given the other minor matters, the Judge may consider taking this into suspended prison sentence territory.

If what you are saying is right, and we can convince the court, the sentence will be a lot lower. I think I will be able to get it down to a maximum two-year ban and some charity shop work. If what I think is correct, then I might get that down even further for you. I believe someone may have stolen your identity and if we can show that to be true you will get a lot of sympathy from this judge.

Take a moment and think, how could someone who you don't know have got hold of all your personal details, more than ten years ago, without your knowledge?"

This wasn't happening. If it wasn't bad enough that Stella was here in the first place, now someone had stolen her identity, and this was going to put her in prison!

Who, how, when, why? Stella thought back.

Then she remembered – V festival. She was there in 2004, the same year she moved into her house. She lost her purse, and her driving licence that was in it, while she was dancing to Amy Winehouse. It was reported to security and the police, but never found. She explained this to David and he looked as though she had given him the answer.

"Great," he said, with a smile. "That sounds like that could be the answer. Let me explain this to the prosecutor. Forget everything else for now. This won't get sorted out today, and I'm afraid you will need to come back here in a couple of weeks. We have some work to do in order to prove this for you. Sloppy police work yet again has led to the wrong set of convictions being sent to the court. The prosecution will have to get your fingerprints checked against the other Stella Green also."

With that David ushered Stella back to the hallway and disappeared back into court. A few minutes later he returned, still smiling, and told Stella she would need to go back in, but not to worry as the Judge would be more sympathetic this time. With that they went back in. Stella back into the glass cage of the dock and David next to the prosecutor looking at Judge Snowdon. David remained on his feet and gestured to Stella to sit down. Clearly he had some clout here as this was the judge's court, not David's. Stella sat.

"Sir," David addressed the judge. "You will recall Miss Green from earlier, identified but no plea taken."

The clerk, replied quick as a shot, "No address either Mr Hughes, we didn't even get that far."

David apologised and gave Stella's address. "Sir, I know the court expects a plea at the earliest opportunity, indeed the Criminal Procedure Rules demand it, but this is one of those rare matters where it may be prudent to adjourn. We may have the wrong defendant in the dock. I am not sure of that statement, but I am sure that this lady is the victim of identity theft. I am convinced she has no previous convictions due to a driving licence theft in 2004. Sir, the Crown will need to check Mrs Green's fingerprints against those of the arrested person and against those held for the lady with the previous convictions appended to her criminal record here today. I believe they will be different. If they are the same, we will have lost two weeks only, but saved a huge amount of trial listing time. If they are different, we can expect this matter to reach a swift conclusion in two weeks. I have spoken with my friend who prosecutes and on this application, we are agreed. With your leave, a two-week adjournment back to your court and currently Mrs Green is on unconditional bail."

The prosecutor nodded his agreement.

Without a pause Judge Snowdon looked at Stella and his face tightened. "Stand up Mrs Green. I was most unimpressed with your antics earlier, but it appears my displeasure may have been misplaced. I am prepared to allow Mr Hughes two weeks to resolve this issue for the reasons he stated. I do not do this lightly.

Rest assured, if, in two weeks' time, I discover that this has been a delaying tactic on your part, the consequences will be a sentence that will act as a deterrent both to you and others for the future.

Back here at nine-thirty in two weeks and unconditional bail. Fail to turn up and you will be going straight to custody. Do you understand me?"

Stella looked petrified, eyes transfixed on the judge, the word 'custody' spinning round her head, and she nodded moments before David got her out of the dock and the court room, just in case the Judge changed his mind.

Outside he told her, "Don't worry about his bark, just stretching his judicial muscles for the crowds. He likes a little play and he didn't mean it. He's actually OK, so long as you aren't pulling his chain. We need to talk later. Is your mobile correct on the charge sheet?"

Again, Stella nodded.

"Good, I'll call you in a day or two when I get five minutes, we need to meet to discuss this further. In the meantime, see if you can dig out any further information regarding the stolen purse. I have another few cases, get out of here, go home and unwind a bit."

With a smile he was gone.

Chapter 2

Stella turned the key in the lock, opened the door, entered and locked it behind her. She headed straight down the hallway and into the kitchen. She opened the wine fridge and poured herself an extremely large glass of her favourite South African white, Secretary Bird – hard to find, amazing to quaff.

En-route to the lounge she managed to lose her shoes. She curled up on the sofa with its overstuffed cushions and modern patterning, took a huge gulp of wine, and started to sob. She looked across the room and took in its emptiness. The large abstract art on the wall contrasting with the sharp lines of the mirror above the wood burner. The wall mounted TV stared blankly back at her. The empty chair where once her husband sat. She once more looked down at the liquid offering temporary solace and with a second mouthful, the glass was empty.

This had been the worst day in her life since Tony, the ex-husband, admitted to the lengthy affair with his secretary. On that occasion she had kicked him hard between the legs, regretting the fact she wasn't wearing shoes, particularly steel toe caps, and threw him out. It was his first and only infidelity, as far as she was aware, and she would not risk another one. Today was different, no one to kick in the nuts except herself. No one to offer sympathy because it was all her own fault. She was the one who got drunk after a Fuckwit (her rather apt pet name for the now historical Tony) debate and had got into her mini the following morning to see her so-called friends at yoga. She never arrived, having been arrested on the way there. Taken to the police investigation centre in Bury St Edmunds where she was placed in a cell. Shortly thereafter, she was taken to another room and went through the rigmarole of providing a breath sample. She had been charged with drink driving and put back in the cell until she gave a reading low enough for the Sergeant to allow her to drive home. She had managed to cover up her absence with a tale of illness, hangover really, but the day of reckoning was coming. She could cycle to her yoga class at Morton Hall and say it was part of an improving health regime, but the truth would worm its way out eventually, it always did. The humiliation would follow. It was all Fuckwit's fault. Had he not been shagging about with that other woman, none of this would have happened.

Stella, still with tears streaming down her face, went back to the kitchen and picked up the bottle. She took it into the living room and refilled her glass. With the next swig she began to think back. She'd had it all, a great life, not wanting financially and a circle of regular friends. She grew up in Bury St Edmunds, an only child. Her father, a well-respected owner of a car dealership that took off in the seventies. He became a franchise operation with several branches throughout East Anglia, selling them all on retirement for an extremely healthy sum to the Jardine Motor Group, who continue to run them to this day. The majority of the money from the sale was put into a trust fund for Stella and any subsequent children. They had a home in the best street in Bury and her mother didn't need to work, although she did, part-time, as a nurse at West Suffolk Hospital. Stella, as a result, was privately educated and one of the first girls in Woodbridge School, some thirty miles and a daily train ride away.

Having completed her A levels, she decided on a business and marketing degree, no doubt spurred on by the vision of her father's success (which was due to luck, good timing, and an ability to sell ice to Eskimos) and a desire to make her own fortune. It was in her second year of university she met Fuckwit. He wasn't Fuckwit then, he was an undergraduate in software engineering looking at a First-Class Honours Degree. He played rugby for the university and Eastern Counties, and was destined for great things. A charmer, handsome and adored by all the ladies. Stella felt the luckiest girl alive when they got together. He had chosen her above all the other girls, and he could have had his pick. At that moment he was to be her man for life. Both would have great jobs and the trappings of wealth would ensure retirement in a cottage on the Norfolk coast. As time went by in her second year, they were spending more and more time together – at the inevitable expense of study. Stella's grades began to slip, but Tony continued to shine – with her and the tutors. This was a *real love* job as far as Stella was concerned and Tony was saying all the right things to her: *"I will look after you; don't worry you won't need to work; I will be the breadwinner for both of us; We are the perfect couple."* Looking back at it now, such was her blindness she never noticed but he never once used the 'L' word.

After they graduated, Tony found a post in a new company, just setting up and trading out of Cambridge. Stella went to work as a PA for a local landscape gardening firm. Her work was more office manager than PA, and she quickly learnt all about running an office, staff issues, scheduling, banking and cash flow. She was good at it too. Her boss, Tom, loved and loathed her. Through her efforts the company profits increased, cash flow looked after itself, but she was very tough on Tom's spending. Those little extras the company always funded, never much individually, but over a year mounting up to many thousands of pounds. This excess she curbed as much as she could, and it paid off. For the first time she looked properly at charge-out rates, one third each for running costs, wages and profit. This allowed for proper job costing and although Tom thought they would be pricing themselves out of work, it didn't happen, because his company's reputation was almost as good as her father's had been. She was also a bill tyrant, chasing fourteen days after a bill was submitted. All of this worked together to change the company from one that was living hand to mouth, to one that began to show signs of real viability and even the prospect of expansion. My, she was a bright and efficient young lady.

Tony was also very intelligent and as the company he worked for developed, so did he. His skills as a software engineer and his ability to charm the clients meant he was better placed in management rather than sitting behind his desk turning out code. He was given a team to look after and he oversaw their work exceptionally well. He would give them ideas on how to solve the problems, monitor their work, and point them in the right direction. They quickly became almost as skilled as he was, which made his life much easier since he could let them get on with it. To avoid him leaving for a rival firm, he was quickly promoted again to director, given all the perks and the PA, the bloody PA. Why a nice pretty one? Why not one with limited personality or little in common with him? But that was for the future.

They were so happy, and Stella and Tony decided a director needed a wife and a family, it was how it was done. As simple as that, marriage it was. Both mothers were against it, and both for the same reason, neither one of the couple had hit thirty. The fathers simply wanted a quiet life.

On the last Saturday in July 1990, they were married. The honeymoon was in Greece for two weeks. On their return, Tony gave her the keys to a new executive house in Thurston, which they would share until the day he left. She had no choice in the home, or anything else come to think of it. With the brilliance and wonder of hindsight, she wished she had put her foot down at that point. But they had a four-bedroom detached house in an up-and-coming area on the outskirts of Bury, life was good.

Tony mentioned family as part of the deal, ah yes, family. Stella loved her job with the little landscaping firm, it gave her purpose, but Tony was insistent. Not ready, but eager to please, Stella found herself pregnant. Mum would look after the child and she would go back to work – sorted. Mum was up for the idea, as was her father, but seven months into the pregnancy Stella came home to be greeted by the police.

"Can we come in please, we need to have a talk?"

"Yes, of course," a puzzled Stella replied. Why would the police want to talk to her?

"Have a seat please Mrs Green, we have some awful news. A few hours ago, a lorry was involved in a collision. The other vehicle was a car, a Vauxhall. There were two occupants in the car. The car belonged to your parents. We are so sorry, but the paramedics could do nothing to save them."

Stella broke down, clutching her ever-expanding stomach, and screamed a scream of the damned, a wailing so loud and powerful it put her into and early labour. Thankfully, six hours later, Brian was born. A day of ultimate sadness mixed seamlessly with ultimate joy. Tony had come to be with her but was as much use in these situations as anyone else without medical experience. He also offered little by way of moral or emotional support. How does one plan for, or deal with, this? Joy in the extreme for a first-born son seems massively disrespectful to the grandparents who would never see the child, or their own daughter again. Tony went for the silent hug as being the best way forward.

Stella struggled with motherhood due to grief, a grief she never recovered from, and a grief that started her drinking. Not excessively, and not on a school night, but enough to act as a crutch for solace. Tony was as good a father as he was a comfort to Stella. He went to work, came home, drank, and started to complain. Stella had changed, and he didn't know how to cope or deal with it.

He said to her, "Where is the girl I wooed, the lady I married?"

She had become depressed and moody and she could tell that he didn't like it.

Despite the difficulties, as time progressed, so did Brian – into a wonderful young man, as bright as his father and just as eager. School was a breeze, he played rugby too – better than his father, sailed through his A Levels, and went to Edinburgh University to study medicine.

Now, Stella was truly alone. Empty. Yes, she had her social life with the *ladies that lunch*, Bury society, where the size of the savings account mattered as much as the last holiday. But it was all just fake, a show for everyone else. These ladies knew of their husbands' dalliances, but the lifestyle was too good to give up. She had massages, waxing and went to yoga, all paid for by Tony. He would never betray her – not like the others.

Oh, how she was mistaken. How could she have been so stupid? How could he be like all the rest? In truth, the hurt inside Stella and its manifestations had ground him down. As he left that was it, he had said?

'His PA was beautiful, younger, made him laugh and showed him attention, attention he had not had for some years. He was only human after all' and 'You weren't supposed to know!'

That dalliance developed into a full-blown affair and as the grass *is always* greener, he succumbed, leaving Stella for his bit of fluff. He didn't tell her, it was his tart's text to him while he was in the shower, which Stella saw as it flicked up on his phone *"really loved you deep inside me this afternoon"* was all she could read. Stella had the good grace (or more probably was in shock and denial) to wait for Fuckwit to exit the shower before she confronted him with the terrible truth. He could not deny it and that night, he packed an overnight bag and left.

Stella downed two bottles that night in her despair. That was three weeks ago, and things had changed. Stella was resigned to the fact she was forty-nine and single, with no income, having given up her job when Brian was born. Sure, things had to be sorted out, but she had to rebuild herself and that is exactly what she would do.

Chapter 3

Stella awoke in the early hours, still curled up on the sofa where she had cried herself to sleep. A streetlight provided the only illumination through the window. Her mind recalled the previous day. Its novelty, its horror. She realised sitting there was going to do her no favours and she must pick herself up and move on. How much did she drink last night? The bottle told her the answer, only half the bottle was left; she would be sober enough in a few hours' time.

With a newfound resolve, she pulled herself from the overstuffed sofa and made her way up the stairs. She discarded her clothes into the laundry basket that sat in the corner of the bedroom and wandered into the en-suite. She turned on the shower. She caught a quick look of herself in the mirror and confirmed the fact that she looked terrible – yesterday's make up, complete with tear runs in her mascara. Her body was still in good shape for her age. She dwelled in the shower longer than she ought, enjoying the rainfall shower head drenching her, purging away yesterday, and refreshing the skin.

    She grabbed a fluffy white towel – her indulgence, not his – wrapped it around herself and lay down on the bed. She closed her eyes once more. She woke sometime later and took a moment to come round, wondering why she was lying on the bed in just a towel. Stella looked at the clock on the bedside table, nine thirty, not too late considering. She transferred to her favourite extra-fluffy robe and took herself downstairs. The Nespresso was just the thing today for a strong coffee to get the brain cells back from to normality. To relax, she turned on the Sonos, and played an '80s classic pop album while she sipped and enjoyed the coffee with its aroma filling her senses back to fully awake.

That solicitor, David... David... David Hughes, yes him. He had been such a help. She really must thank him for yesterday. What would have happened had he not been there? Heaven knows. He gave her his card, yes, it's in her bag. She moved through the dining room and into the lounge, to find her bag that had been discarded the previous day. Reaching in she took out his card and looked at it. *'David Hughes – Solicitor'* with an address, email and phone number. A pleasantly designed card with an air of sophistication. She would ring and thank him.

She called the number and it rang six times before going to answer machine. Nervously she spoke, "Err, hello, it's Stella Green here, you won't remember me, but you helped me yesterday and I wanted to thank you. You have my number and I hope to speak with you in a few days about what happened and where we go from here."

Well, now she would have to simply wait.

Since the separation three weeks ago, nothing had been resolved – she hadn't heard from her husband at all. So, as far as she was concerned, it was business as usual and everything on the credit card. She had continued with her *ladies that lunch*, massages, waxing (now due) and shopping for one at Waitrose. Today was to be no different, after all she was not off the road yet. Today it was a yoga class at the Self Centre at eleven. Stella returned upstairs, the robe came off and the sports bra and Lycra went on. She hurriedly did her hair and makeup, the mirror on the dressing table revealed a much better sight than yesterday. Stella collected her yoga mat from the bottom of the wardrobe, and jumped into the mini convertible.

Getting into the car she felt nervous. She had a drink yesterday, but was sure, having checked the bottle, she hadn't had that much, and it must be through her system. What if she was seen by the police and stopped? Did her yoga buddies know she had been in court yesterday? Were they all laughing at her? She need not have worried, the drive to the Self Centre was uneventful, even if she felt foolish holding up the traffic behind driving strictly to the speed limit. When she got to class all her yoga buddies were there and a nice gentle flow class was scheduled with Carol. It was just what she needed. Relaxing, she soon found herself back in her old reality, none of the class knew about yesterday, or if they did no one was saying.

After a shower at the centre and a quick change, Stella headed into town, parking as she always did at Ram Meadow. It was the cheapest car park in town, the bays were small, but it was a lovely steady uphill walk into the town centre. It also gave a great view of the town as she went past the war memorial and up Angel Hill.

"Hey, Stella!" Came the familiar voice of Trudy as she turned into the Butter market. "How are you?"

"Hi Trudy, good to see you. You look awesome!"

In reality, Trudy didn't look awesome, she never did. Age was against her and far too many holidays in the sun had left her skin looking ten years older than her true age. That, and a poor lip fill recently done at the local 'specialist' (a word used for expensive) clinic.

After the usual small talk and general gossip, the Bury society thrive on, it was decided that they would have a quick lunch in Café Rouge. They were ushered to a seat in the rear courtyard, small, with uncomfortable chairs, but at least there was sunlight and fresh air.

Over a chicken Caesar salad, Stella endured Trudy telling her all about which husband was having sex with who and where, when they were next going abroad, how much the holiday was costing, the new car they were looking at and that they were thinking of buying a yacht. It was an ordeal that Stella did not want to go through, all Trudy really wanted was the latest gossip on how she was coping after Tony. Any information Stella gave to Trudy would be round the whole sorry lot of them before she got home, and it was none of their nosey business. Stella simply confirmed everything was fine, and she delighted in having the whole bed to herself and never having to put the toilet seat down. She deliberately chose not to mention yesterday!

"Great to see you Trudy, we must all do lunch and a spa together soon," were her departing words, although she had little enthusiasm to fulfil them. It was a relief when she left Trudy, and Stella gave a sigh once she was in the clear.

Stella spent the next few hours mooching in her favourite shops, looking for things to spend Tony's money on. So many independent shops, although the numbers were dwindling. The market square was also full of great architecture. Stella always had her head looking up at the rooflines. How she never bumped into anyone was a mystery. She had been quite successful in her spending over the last two weeks. Several hundred on new underwear, all fitted, in Cambridge. Several hundred more in John Lewis and some new jewellery courtesy of Thurlow and Champness. It probably totalled around £3000, and she knew she would have to face the music when he checked the credit card statement. Stella didn't care, she was his wife and he would have to provide for her. For the moment it made her smile, that small act of revenge. All she had in her own name was the £2000 a month income from the trust fund, and about £5000 she had managed to hide away over the years that she had saved for Christmas, birthdays etc. For the time being at least, she could survive and also enjoy the spending.

Tired, she went home.

En-route she recalled that it was always lonely going home knowing that once the door was shut it would remain so with no one else coming through it. Another sigh expressed her deflated feeling. Stella was OK on her own when she knew her husband was coming home, but he wasn't and each time the door closed it reminded her of that fact. It made the house seem somehow colder and she shivered. It was a fact she would like never to have had to come to terms with. His death would have been easier to cope with somehow than the knowledge another lover had replaced her.

She went inside and took her new purchases with her, carefully removed the tags and folding or hanging as appropriate. The drawers were now certainly getting full and wardrobe space was becoming a premium. Stella changed into more comfortable jogging bottoms and a loose T-shirt then returned downstairs and into the kitchen. Having made a cup of tea, (Yorkshire – nice and strong) she went back to the living room and put the news on. She made herself comfortable on the sofa, back leaning against one of the arms. Brexit, more London stabbings and the Trump saga, how depressing was that?

Music. Yes, let's have some music to chill out with. "Alexa, play some light jazz." Alexa obeyed.

As the jazz played and soothed her mind, she relaxed with

her tea. Stella began to think about the future. She would have to learn to live on her own, sod the Bury society, and make new friends. Friends who were true, who valued her for herself, not for her wealth and designer clothing. She would learn to dance. She was fit enough and young enough.

"*Always fancied having a go at ballroom,*" she mused. "*Ah, no partner. Salsa, that was sexy and with her legs, bound to get noticed.*" Her musings continued, and she decided she better eat before it got too late. Jacket potato and a side salad. She prepared it and sat at the breakfast bar, jazz still audible from the living room, and enjoyed every morsel. As the jazz and food eased her mind and body, she decided on a bath.

Upstairs Alexa continued as the bath ran. Bubbles and sod it, as an extra treat, bath salts; she had earned it today. As she sank deep into it, again her thoughts turned towards the future. She could do this; she didn't need a man to let her down. Sure, a companion and some sex would be good, but not vital to survival and happiness. How long would he continue to fund her credit card? What are the costs of running the house? She would deal with that in the morning. For now, the bath was all she needed, and it made her. Stella lay there listening to the music and watched the clouds gently pass by the bathroom window. Her breathing was steady and relaxed. Pure innocent relaxation – she needed a massage: get it booked, another tomorrow job. Once the water was nearly cold, Stella removed herself from the bath reluctantly and towelled herself dry. She got into bed and pulled the duvet up high keeping in the warmth that still remained in her body after the bath. She turned on the TV, put on a film, and fell asleep.

The next day was Friday, of little consequence except that it was the day the Bury Free Press was published, of little use save for the scandal in its pages to satiate the appetites of Bury society. Page 7, page bloody 7! There it was, Stella's name and street in black and white for the world (well, Bury society) to see. Her heart sank and her body grew tense. A shudder ran from the top of her head to the tips of her toes. In disbelief, she read it again, slowly and nervously. How long would it take?

The answer was not long. Stella made her breakfast. She sat at the breakfast bar watching the news, trying to focus on anything except page 7. She finished her avocado on toast and went through the routine of taking a shower and getting dressed. Going nowhere today, she was content with minimal make up (never none), a T-shirt and today her favourite Levi's, tired but tight. It was late as she was in no rush and at nine-forty-five a.m. it started.

The first call was the worst, Tony's mother. One of the society elders, considerably richer and better than thou, (although only in her head) a matriarchal figure in the society, to be feared. Her word was law and boy did she enjoy the scandal.

"Oh my god Stella, is this story true?" and without pausing for breath, "You poor soul, are you all right, what happened? Can we help?"

Each question was actually a rephrasing of the same one when Miriam asked it. She was really saying, *"Holy shit this is a great scandal and proves my boy was right for leaving you. Tell me what you have done so I can slander you across town, ruining any social standing you have, and have you shunned by all."*

Totally ashamed, Stella confirmed, through gritted teeth and a tense body, she had been caught drinking and driving. She explained the circumstances of the night before, although this she bet would never get to the society's ears. She went on to describe the stolen driving licence and the humiliation. The journalist had commented on her collapse in the dock, since that was rare and gave the story more impact, more lines, more kudos. It made for a better story, but was far more embarrassing for its victim.

That was it, Stella was soon to be friendless, yes, they would nod and put up the pretence of friendship in public, but the phone calls, invitations, socials and spa days would all dry up very soon. At this moment it seemed the universe had conspired against her and there was nothing she could do. By the end of the call, Stella felt thoroughly humiliated.

Of course, Trudy called, and not too long after Miriam. "Stella you never said," same question, different words.

"How could I? Seriously, this is just completely mortifying and it's all down to Fuckwit." Yes, she had now renamed her husband to the society, she may as well go straight to the society undertakers. She really was going to be dead to them.

Next was Sue, then Chrissy and Jane, all the same questions just using different words. "*ENOUGH!*" She unplugged the phone and, although it was half an hour before wine o'clock officially started (midday in many households), she poured a large pinot for comfort. Change the record, move on, move on again, get through, survive, grow strong and show the bloody lot of them!

She planned last night to make a start and that's what she would do. Finances. Let's see where we are. Stella went through the meticulous files she kept (a hangover from her training) and very soon had created a new spreadsheet.

Outgoings. It had everything in it. Insurances, utilities, food, holidays, birthdays, Christmas, entertaining. The spreadsheet even averaged each annual expense in the year and broke it down to a monthly spend. She looked at the bottom line, total annual spend: £32,000. She hadn't realised, but the credit card subsidised her existence. OK, let's make the cuts, remove the excess, trim the fat. £28,000, she was closer. Stella removed the car running costs which took her down to £25,000.

She was skint, or she would be when Tony got the credit card bill. Worse, she would be bankrupt in five months and left with no savings! Now was the time to consider things, work things out, make plans, but what? Last night she was going to take up dancing, not any more she wasn't. Stella spent some time just staring blankly at the spreadsheet.

The task of creating and compiling the spreadsheet took her most of the afternoon and mentally wore her out. She plugged the phone back in and, with her wine, curled on the sofa to chill. Barely five minutes and the bloody phone rang again.

This time it was Tony.

"Hi Stella, look I know you are still probably pretty pissed off with me and probably don't want to talk to me right now, especially if what Mum has told me is true, but we need to talk." She gritted her teeth.

"What do you want?" Stella snarled, through drink and self-pity, not thinking that she needed to keep him sweet for as long as possible.

"Look Stella, you know I keep a constant check on the cash flow with the banking app. I checked it again this morning. I've seen the size of the credit card bill. You know it's in my name and I have to pay it. Frankly, I can't do this and keep my new place up. Something has to give. I wanted to give you more time and more notice, but yesterday you went too far, three grand, what were you thinking?"

She knew she had gone too far but hey. She forgot he checked the app at least daily, god she hated technology today, phones and banking apps. "Look, I am sorry." she couldn't use his name she was so furious. "I met Trudy and we went a little overboard. It won't happen again."

"Three grand is more than a little. I can't afford you like this, Stella. You have left me no choice, tomorrow I'm taking you off the card, you'll have to cope on your trust fund. Take care, bye."

And with that the bastard hung up. Stella stared at the phone, now silent. How dare he! What am I supposed to do? Shunned by society and now destitute (well in her own mind anyway).

Five minutes later she decided on minor revenge, the card is hers until tomorrow! Hoorah for technology this time. The internet. Where shall I go? Kenya, a safari, excellent idea, but I will need to relax afterwards. Yes, that's the way forward. Within an hour and with a feeling very satisfied with herself, it was booked. Three months to wait before she went away. The great migration would be on, and two weeks chasing them and hunting the big five would be a nice break. Relaxing in Zanzibar on the beach for a week after sounded idyllic. It was six grand, but she wasn't paying and it served him right for his appalling timing. Then she ordered the clothing, sweat repelling bush toned clothes and a new camera. Tony would go mad, but basically tough shit. She couldn't wait. Once it was all done, Stella sat back in the chair and smiled to herself. That act of defiance felt good.

Now for a really hard conversation – her son. Brian would not be impressed. He would find the spending hilarious, but really mother, drink-driving. But he would support her. The phone rang and Brian picked up.

"Hi Mum, I know, dad rang earlier. You all right? Need me home? Yes, I think you have been stupid but hey, it happens."

All said before she could say one word. "Oh Brian, you are such a joy, yes to everything except no I don't need you home. As long as you are at the end of the phone if needed, I'll be fine.

Thank you."

They were on the phone nearly an hour and it was a wonderful, loving mother/son conversation. It was needed. After it was done Stella felt a little better, but not totally.

She'd had enough of today and couldn't be bothered to run a bath. A quick shower and a chick flick in bed with a cup of tea would do the trick. She did, it did. Stella slept.

Chapter 4

Stella's former Saturday routine was domestic in nature. It was her cleaning and shopping day, and this had not changed, even given recent events. She woke and, as normal, took a quick shower. More jeans and a sloppy old T-shirt, no bra, and no war paint. She went downstairs and made some fresh orange juice in the juicer. Then she cooked herself some eggs which she enjoyed on some granary toast with crushed avocado, her latest favourite but also healthy and energy giving. She checked her mobile – nothing new, excellent.

With some vigour as always, she set about the task of cleaning top to bottom. As there was no one to cause any real mess the task was not overly arduous, and her belief was the sooner I start, the sooner it's done. She had a copy of *Hinch yourself Happy* and had picked out the best bits, or the bits that suited her some months earlier. Stella loved to Hinch away her Saturday morning. So, with a variety of dusters, cloths and made-up bottles of Hinch standard cleaning liquids, she was away. First her bathroom, twenty minutes later – sparkling. A light dusting of the bedroom and landing, the same for the other three bedrooms and bingo, upstairs done. Vacuum the stairs, wipe the banister and just the ground floor to do. Lounge, kitchen, dining room, utility and study and in two hours flat she was done, she had broken a sweat but that was normal. She relaxed with a coffee and noticed a missed call on her phone. There was a message from a number she didn't recognise. Curious, Stella dialled and listened:

"Hi Stella, I hope it's still OK to call you that? It's David Hughes here. Sorry I didn't get back to you sooner, but other work matters have had me tied up for the last two days. I work on my own and so the weekend is the best time to catch up with administration, unless I need to attend the Saturday remand court or police station. I'm waffling, sorry. I don't know what your plans are today, but if you're available we could meet up and have a chat about where we go from here, assuming you still want me to represent you, that is? If you pick this up give me a call and we can fix something up, today if possible."

Stella normally went to Sainsbury or Waitrose on a Saturday afternoon and popped into town for the butchery items. Today, however, priorities were somewhat different, and she needed to get this mess sorted out sooner rather than later. She called David back. This time he answered.

"Hi David, it's Stella, sorry I missed your call."

"Stella, great. Sorry it's short notice but the way I run my business means most things are done when they can be slotted in. I don't like seeing clients at the weekend but I know my diary is crammed next week and your case is important, if you still need my help?"

Without thinking, Stella replied, "Yes, I would love you to continue to help me out. When and where shall we meet?"

"Well, I live in Bury, my office is a lock up on the Moreton Hall estate, so wherever suits you and I have no plans presently. We need to be a little private for your confidentiality though. I can come to you, Thurston isn't it? Or we could meet in town? I'm trying to think of somewhere in town that's quiet."

"How about we grab a take-away coffee from Caffé Nero, and we can chat in the Abbey Gardens? The benches are set apart so it would be sort of private."

"Great idea. Shall we say an hour outside Café Nero?"

"Make it an hour and a half, I need to get ready."

"No need to dress up for me, see you in an hour and a half."

Shit, no need to dress up, what to wear? She was not about to be seen in town looking a mess, especially with another man. Secretly Stella hoped she would be seen by at least one of the society ladies. It would soon get about she was in the company of another man. Miriam and Tony would seethe, it was hilarious. Yes, need to look good, even if one plus one wasn't two in this case. They didn't need to know that, did they?

Straight upstairs Stella had another shower and put on her new underwear, simply because it fitted superbly. She opened the wardrobe door and looked at her skirts hanging on the rail. Flicking her way through them. *'No, no, no, hmmm, no, this one'.* She chose a skirt, above the knee of course, one from Javelin, a local independent that everyone knew was a bit snobby but had great stuff. Then her attention went to the rail above, in order to find a blouse. Having performed the same ritual as she had with the skirt, she chose a blouse from Gant. It was one of her favourites and suited her figure. Tights and short boots – done. She made-up her face taking years off her, such was her expertise with foundation and a brush, and she was ready. A little jewellery and Gucci handbag, into the car and off she went.

Stella parked in Ram Meadow and walked purposefully up Angel Hill towards Café Nero, which was halfway up. She was looking around to see who she could see and in doing so couldn't help but notice, once more, how beautiful that part of town looked, mostly medieval and simply a quaint market town.

David was waiting outside, and you couldn't miss the double take as he saw Stella walking up the hill. His eyes went from top to bottom and then slowly back to the top. Unprofessional but understandable. Stella was proud of how she looked, and she made the best of it, especially today, but not for David's benefit.

"Hi Stella, let me get the coffee, what can I get you?"

"Just a latte please, David." Stella noticed Jane was in the window seat with her husband and two kids, she hadn't noticed her – she would! As David turned to go inside, she followed in close proximity. As soon as she was inside the door she looked straight at Jane and cheekily said, "Hi Jane, I didn't expect to see you here. I can see you're with your family, so I won't intrude. Oh, by the way, this is David. David, Jane. Jane, David."

Jane's eyes were wide, and Stella swore her mouth dropped open for at least three seconds. "Err, err, hi Stella, and hi David. Nice to meet you."

David simply replied, "And nice to meet you too." Judging by the look on David's face he must have been thinking, what the hell has just happened there. There was a curious atmosphere created by the surprise and unnecessary conversation, evident in Jane's response. Inside Stella was wetting herself with laughter, it could not have been more perfectly executed.

David dutifully bought the coffee and as they walked out and down Angel Hill Stella snuck a glimpse at Jane. She was taking in every aspect of David: his polished shoes, the smart jeans she swore were Armani, the shirt, which can only have been a Trotter and Dean (the most exclusive independent tailor in the town for years). They were a similar age and the ladies would want to know all the details. Who was he? full description, were they in a relationship? what did he do? Anything Jane knew would be assumed and, what she thought she knew, was mostly wrong. It could not have started any better for her, that meeting.

They crossed the road and walked under the gate into the

Abbey Gardens. The gardens were beautifully kept and looked stunning all year round. Stella chose a seat in the central avenue, hoping to be further noticed by any of the society that may pass. They sat a sensible distance apart and placed their respective coffees between them creating a barrier, professional for David, impulsive and guarded for Stella.

David started, "What the hell was that about?"

"Don't worry, I may tell you later. Now let's get this nightmare sorted out and thank you for seeing me."

David was in the close proximity of a beautiful woman and wanted to maintain his professional position, but it was difficult. It was difficult to stay focussed on her eyes and not let his own wander. He was not used to this given his usual clients, heroin riddled, on benefits, kids in care, tattoos and swore like the ungrateful bastards they were, and that was just the women! He could smell her perfume, no idea what it was, but he was thoroughly taken in by its scent. *Get real David, this is just a client and you can't go there.*

"OK," he said, "business."

They talked about the case, Stella's eyes darting left and right trying to make sure no one could overhear and also looking for any more of the society. It was decided that Stella needed to provide more information about the loss of her purse, and may have to go back to the police station to provide her fingerprints again. She had no problem with this. David started to talk about costs – his – and legal aid. He explained that the previous court hearing was free, as was today, but after that the meter starts running.

Legal aid wasn't going to happen, with the trust fund money her income was too high. David confirmed that it could be as much as £2,000 if things weren't resolved at the next hearing.

Stella was now on a budget, she didn't have that money spare, her savings would have to be spent sensibly and not wasted on a fat-cat lawyer. No wonder they all had brand new cars! Stella told David about her position, the recent separation, the trust fund income, the savings, and the house she now had to fund and run by herself. She told him she would need to find a job, and that would be difficult given the number of years that she had been out of work. Yes, she was good, but she was rusty, and her age was now against her. To make it harder, she would be up against all these young adults fresh from university who were unable to get jobs and would take anything to gain experience.

David asked her about her past jobs and the experience she had. She told him truthfully. He admitted that things might be difficult for her and appreciated her position.

"Let me think about it. I'll see if I can find a way round our problem," he said. David wanted to help, but he was not a charity. They finished their coffee and called an end to the meeting. David left with a shake of the hand and said he would be in touch.

She watched him walk through the abbey gate and back towards town, he didn't look back. Christ, what now? David was supposed to make things easier, but his fees were too much and right now she couldn't justify it. Stella didn't feel like hanging around, so she left the Abbey Gardens by the side gate and drove her car home. The day was running away with her now and she didn't fancy having to do Sainsbury's. Her motivation was low, as was her energy. She decided to sit in the lounge and listen to more jazz. Within half an hour she felt her head dropping. God, was she really dozing on a Saturday afternoon? That wasn't her at all. All she could think of was the court hearing, she would have to go there herself to face that bully of a judge again. Why would he listen to her, she was just another defendant, another criminal trying to blag her way to freedom, just like the rest of the posse. Would she end up like them? Cheering the freedom of her new mates? Cursing the court and the system? All these thoughts, none of them positive. And now she had to find work, but where, she would be unable to drive soon when the Judge banned her. Where could she work? How would she bring any money in?

Her phone rang, an unknown number.

"Hi Stella, it's David. I have had an idea how we can solve your temporary cash flow crisis, something for our mutual benefit."

Intriguing! "Hi, David, how do you suggest I do that?"

"Not so fast Stella. I'll tell you but I would like to do it face to face. It's not something I normally do, but if you would meet me for dinner we can discuss it, what do you say?"

What? Is this lawyer hitting on me? I am not laying on my back to pay his bloody bill. "I don't know, the sound of this does not make me feel comfortable," She replied with some trepidation.

"Seriously Stella, it's all above board and I have honourable intentions. Dinner, no strings, we talk. If you like what I have to say great, if not, you've had a free dinner. I thought we could try the Angel Hotel."

Right, we'll be seen by more society, of that I am sure. "You are on, say eight?"

"Eight it is. See you there."

Stella decided that she ought to put David's number in her contacts.

What was this day all about? This was not her normal Saturday and was changing by the minute. Three hours to get herself ready and back to town it was. A quick soak in the bath, washing and shaving her legs and bikini line (not that he was going to get the benefit of that). Once more she found herself at her dressing table re-applying the war paint, making herself look exceptional, make up to match the dress she had picked out, calf length with a split nearly to the top of her thigh, red with black embroidery on it, sophisticated, smart and sexy all at the same time. Her jewellery was simple and contemporary, and her shoes matched perfectly, patent red leather Jimmy Choo's. Why did she have butterflies in her stomach? She didn't even know if she liked him. It had been such a long time since she had been in the company of another man for dinner, that was it.

Once more David was waiting for her to arrive, this time in the foyer of the Angel Hotel, he shook her hand. The maître d' led them to a table at the front of the hotel by the window overlooking Angel Hill car park and across to the Abbey Gardens entrance they had walked through earlier. Stella could people watch if the conversation dried up. They sat, and David poured them both a drink of water.

"I just made an assumption."

"Perfect."

They studied the menu and both decided to skip a starter. Monkfish for Stella, Belly pork for David.

"Ok David, what's this plan of yours?" Stella asked. She looked at him, properly, for the first time. He was fairly easy on the eye, he scrubbed up well, was clean, didn't smell, hair was blonde, not receding and he had wonderful Daniel Craig-blue eyes. Yes, attractive and sophisticated.

David began to explain, "I'm a lawyer who works on my own. As you know, I am crazy busy. I run my own office in Moreton Hall, more a lock up than an office, nothing flash but cheap to rent. I used to have more staff, solicitors and so on, but with all the cuts to funding rates it became difficult and we had to downsize. Long story short, I ended up on my own in the business and trying to run the place without help. I work constantly trying to keep up with everything, all the regulations, getting the billing done, keeping the clients happy, being in court and the police station. I have many regular clients, but the money I earn from Legal Aid these days barely brings in enough and I'm missing out on work because I simply don't have the time given the paperwork that's needed."

"So, you're overworked. All that means is, I don't get the service you want me to pay for. Don't take that the wrong way but £2,000 is a lot of money for someone who hasn't got the time to do the job properly."

"No offence taken, and that is precisely my point. Not only you, but my other clients too. I'm winging most of what I do and it's only my reputation that allows me to get away with it. This is where you come in. As I see it, at the moment I have too much work and I'm losing money as a result. It's only a matter of time before this all comes crashing down when I miss something serious. Then there's you. You told me of all your experience in management earlier over coffee. You're mature enough not to be going off on maternity leave and you need work. I have a bill for you and you can't justify paying it in your head."

Stella was listening intently and now catching on to what was coming.

"In a few weeks you won't be able to drive for at least a year, and you need something local. You live in Thurston. I like your personality and I think you could organise me. What I'm suggesting is that you work for me on a month's trial without pay. This will cover your bill. You can organise me, my diary, get the finances up to date and run the office with a staff of one, that's you by the way. It'll free me up to do more work that earns me money and, if after a month we both see the benefits, we can formalise things properly. What do you think?"

Stella was interested but needed time to think. "I like the idea, but not sure it would work. It would mean turning my life upside down even more than it recently has been."

"I don't want an answer now, just have a think. It'll help us both out."

The meal arrived and quietly, they ate. Both of them were wondering about the full implications of what David had proposed. Stella was petrified by the thought of taking on this responsibility.

"David, I am worried. I've been out of the office environment for a very long time now, I'm well out of practice. You'll be disappointed and I'll make mistakes. Then I'll feel stupid and frankly, worse than I do now."

"I understand all that, which is why I'm suggesting one month. You have a lot to learn, but I can see something in you that tells me you are both smart and hard working. One month, no lawyers bill and see if you prove me right?"

Stella pondered a moment longer before saying, "OK David, I'll give it a go, and thank you. But I can't start on Monday. Can you give me a week to get myself organised?"

"Of course, I can. See you a week Monday at nine, at the office. I'll get my stuff covered for the morning so I can show you the ropes."

On that note, they parted ways, Stella thanking David once more at the door with a peck on the cheek. Stella sat in her car for at least ten minutes, a thousand thoughts spiralling through her head. Was this her new future? It was certainly the start of it at any rate. She had forgotten all about being seen by the society and didn't know if she had or hadn't.

Chapter 5

Stella woke on Sunday morning after a restful sleep. The best sleep she'd had for the last three weeks. She put on her joggers and a T-shirt and went to the kitchen, poured herself a large glass of fresh orange and sat at the breakfast bar. She held the glass up to her lips and stared at the wall before her, deep in thought. Yesterday had been a crazy day, she mused. She had let the society believe she had a new man, even had dinner with him, and found employment, yes, with him. What a day it was. A roller coaster of emotions but, on balance, she thought, a satisfying day that gave her some semblance of a real future without Tony. It was with some satisfaction that she took her first mouthful, allowing the sharpness of the orange to tantalise her tastebuds before swallowing. A savouring moment.

Thinking about the day ahead she realised she still needed to go to Sainsbury's and get the weekly shop done. The butchers wouldn't be open and so, Sainsbury's for the meat too. It's not as good as St John Street butchers but would have to do. After a refreshing shower, she got herself ready, replacing her joggers with jeans, and set off in the car. It was uneventful, thankfully, and she pulled into the car park. She had her pick of spaces and parked her car where it would stay in the shade. The store was not very busy, in no time she was round the store and packing everything into the car. Stella thought about filling up with petrol and then realised that she probably would not need a full tank for the foreseeable future. It was only a five-minute drive before she was back home putting everything away. The cupboards were always well stocked and Stella kept them neat and tidy. Dry goods were carefully emptied into plastic containers and returned to their place on the shelf. Tins to the back, to make sure the older stock was used first. The Glass fruit bowl that sat on the island refreshed. It didn't take her long.

She sat down to read the Sunday paper and received a call from her son. It made her smile when she saw his name on the screen before answering. He was a good boy and in regular contact, but not so regular as to be a nuisance. Stella told him about Tony and the credit card, he laughed at his mother's stupidity, and then she told him about her job. He was amazed, he had never known his mother to work, all she had done was look after him. He was, as ever, fully supportive and said if she needed anything he could get down for a week to help. Stella confirmed she was fine and he should concentrate on his studies, they were important. They said their goodbyes. Stella did miss him and wished he would come home, especially now she was on her own, but she did appreciate his need to study and get his qualifications, which would set him up for life. Stella hung up the call and glanced once more at the screen before setting it down on the table.

Feeling hungry, Stella made herself a bagel for lunch and sat in front of the TV to watch an old film on Amazon Prime. She really loved being able to sit in peace and watch films, drama and real-life were her passion. Now she was without Tony, it enabled her mind to switch off, albeit temporarily, from the hurt that was still in her heart and also the emptiness of the house. Today she went for the classic *Fatal Attraction*. It was her favourite film and had seen it many times. This time, however, she imagined the film as her future self-seeking revenge on Tony and the girlfriend.

It was mildly satisfying, especially with a glass of chilled pinot.

Shortly after the film finished the doorbell rang, a Westminster chime that she hated but Tony insisted on – she must remember to change it. She wasn't expecting anyone, no one ever really came over uninvited or unannounced and she wasn't expecting any deliveries from Amazon. She opened the door and her jaw dropped open, anger, rage, love, heartbreak hit all at the same time and in no order.

"What the fuck are you doing here? You don't live here anymore."

"Technically it's still my house and I still have a key," was the reply, which did nothing except to anger Stella some more.

Her jaw tensed and her fingers tightened their grip on the door handle. The door slammed shut, quite how it missed him is a mystery, but he was lucky – this time.

Through the still closed door, came a more effective response, "Stella, I'm sorry, I didn't mean that the way it sounded. Please can I come in, so we can have a civil conversation without all the bloody neighbours listening in and watching for a fight?"

Stella opened the door once again and beckoned him in with a flick of her head, her face still showing her anger at him. It was the first time she had seen him since he left. Part of her wanted to lock the door and never let him go again. The other part wanted to murder him in the kitchen, chop up the body and stick it in the freezer then deny all knowledge he was there. Neither of these thoughts were ever going to be a reality, but Stella thought them anyway. He went through to the lounge and sat in the chair – his chair. It was as though he had never left, except for the atmosphere, cold and nervy with a mild splash of ready-to-boil-over anger.

"Look Stella, we need to talk and I thought I best do it face to face."

"Oh my god, you've gone and got the tart pregnant. That's hilarious, you stupid, cock-led moron."

"No, Stella, I have not. I wanted to talk about us. We have a whole mess that needs to be sorted out, and yes, I have seen the holiday booking. Where the hell are you going?"

Stella felt a bit guilty about the holiday she'd booked in anger the other day, but she also wanted to chuckle at getting this last act of revenge. "That's none of your business Tony. Yes, I booked it when you told me you were cutting me off from the credit card. OK, it was a bit childish, but I was angry with you, I still am. What exactly is it you want to talk about?"

"Well, we need to make sure everything is OK for Brian and we need to resolve the finances, short-term anyway. I'm running two households now and, to be honest, even my director's salary isn't going to keep everything going. Something is going to have to give soon. I was hoping I could support you for a few months and sort this out later once the dust has settled, but we're now talking eight grand on the credit card and there are still running costs. You still have your trust fund income; I am trying to cope on my director's salary. I've rented a place in Cambridge, one of those new apartments in the city, so I can commute to work easily enough, but you know how expensive those places are and then there are my living costs."

"You can't play the poor man with me, Tony. Don't forget, I gave up work for you. I only have the trust fund income and I have to run this house. You're the one who screwed up, not me, and I don't see why I should be financially penalised for your errant penis! You earn far more than my trust fund. You should have rented somewhere cheaper, and I don't see why I should suffer because you're spending money on the tart either. You owe me, nearly twenty-five years we have been married, and I have done everything for you, been a faithful and dutiful wife, given up my career. I will not allow you to take away my future simply because it doesn't suit you anymore. You'll need to, no, have to, support me financially for the rest of my life."

"Look Stella, I'm not here for a row or to start the blame game for this marriage going tits up, but it does take two to tango as it were. I'm happy for you to stay in the house and keep all the equity, hell sell it and get some spare cash. I'll keep my salary, bonus and shares, and savings, and we can call it quits. Fair enough?"

"No Tony, not fair enough. You're letting me have the house, worth about £600k, while you keep your huge salary, whatever savings you have, your bonus and dividend? Don't play me for a fool. Within five years you'll have recouped that and be quids in, and that's before we even think about that great pension you always spoke about. I will not settle for less than half your pension, the house, 20k lump sum from your savings and £1500 per month for ten years. Agree to that and we don't need to investigate your finances. Don't agree and you have an almighty fight on your hands."

"Stella, love, I can't afford that. Sue has a kid of her own and I've promised them Florida later this year. She wants to start riding, and then there's my social life. That would bleed me dry."

"She shouldn't have started by riding you! I have no sympathy for you. I am your wife and you will support me and Brian over that tart and brat, simples. Now, leave your key on the hall table as you leave. Don't you dare come back here at any point or I will not be responsible for my actions. And one last thing, don't you ever call me love again. I am not your love, I thought I was but was sadly mistaken. Now fuck off, you fuckwit." There she'd called him it, now he knew.

Stella had never been this angry in front of Tony. She hoped he would leave immediately or she may physically assault him. Thankfully, it seemed, he got the message. Tony left the house, without his keys. He walked, well nearly ran, out of the house and drove away in his car without looking back.

Stella waited until he was gone, she shook with the rage inside her. She went to the hall took his keys and locked the door. Stella collapsed onto the sofa, pulled her knees up tight to her chest and sobbed. It seemed like an age before the tears finally stopped rolling down her cheeks in rivers of sadness and anger. *How could he discard me on the scrap heap and trade me in for a newer model? Well, my part exchange would be more than he was offering right now. Renting in Cambridge, what a joke, we talked about buying a flat there many times over the years, good for work and weekends at the theatre.* The tart wouldn't go to the theatre, Stella was sure of that. A look in the bathroom mirror scared the life out of her, mascara streaking lines down her face, like *The Scream* and *Psycho* rolled into one. She needed to get out of the house.

She decided to leave the house and get some air, Stella fixed her face and set off for the pub. It took a little longer than usual, with the puffy eyes and mascara streaks, but with skill she managed it. She looked again, *'that's better'*. The Fox was nearest, a bit livelier with a younger crowd, but it was simply company she needed. It was only a ten-minute walk and the fresh air filled her lungs making her feel better with each step away from the house. For nearly the first time in her life, she walked into a pub on her own. The Fox was her local, and she had been there with Tony numerous times. They often had live bands – some of them were quite good. She was on nodding terms with a few of the regulars, but nothing more than that.

Stella ordered a large pinot and soda from the bar and sat at a corner table on her own taking in the comings and goings. A nod from the paedo (not that she knew he was, he just looked like one) whom she raised her glass to, a smile from Mrs Dogwalker, again, dutifully returned. In the opposite corner, some old boys were playing cribbage. They made her chuckle, all flat caps and sugar beet but barely a brain cell of sociability between them.

Stella felt peckish and although the food wasn't brilliant, she went to the bar. "What's the best on offer today then?"

"It's all good, but our homemade burgers are going a storm today."

"OK then, a cheeseburger with salad but no dressing please, oh, and another spritzer."

Taking the spritzer back to her seat, she noticed a small group of young lads come in. They looked like young trouble and smelt of herbal substances. This is why she didn't go down The Fox more often, young bucks smoking weed, and driving on it too. No one did anything about them, just me who gets done. They were always so loud too. Foul-mouthed idiots with a deep Suffolk accent. Mostly labourers or warehouse operatives from round about who got together to abuse Fosters, (why does anyone drink that?) and treat the pub as if they owned it, much to the disgust of the older clients. The old boys gave up on their crib, left the pegs in and returned the board to behind the bar. They would finish their game another day but they were off home. There had been trouble caused by youngsters in the past and the older clientele didn't want to be around if it did kick off. Mrs Dogwalker was off as well.

Stella ate her food and spent her time looking out of the window. She could see the roundabout and the railway bridge. She watched the cars and bikes come and go, always careful at that roundabout and then putting their foot down, they exit to get some exhaust echo from the bridge. Watching others in their daily lives was somehow therapeutic. Imagining the walkers, some with dogs, some with children, Stella looked and gave them nicknames too, decided on their jobs, holidays, sex lives and happiness. Once she had finished what was a great burger, Stella finished off her spritzer and left. She walked slowly up the hill back to her home and again took in huge lungful of air, embracing the freshness of the countryside.

Sitting on the sofa it hit her. This time next week would be her last evening before work. What a scary thought that was. She would need to get everything prepared the night before and would set the alarm so she wasn't late. How would it go? What would David have for her to do? Could she do it? Was she just setting herself up for a fall? *'Stop it Stella, you have enough to worry about that's real without worrying about what may never happen.'*

The phoned pinged – a message – Tony. What now, hadn't he done enough today? Anger rose in her once more. She opened it:

'Stella, I want to apologise, the last thing I wanted to do was have us at each other's throats. I will transfer £1000 per month to your bank account until we get this all resolved, it really is the best I can do. Please let's try and get on, T'

She could just about survive financially now but would still need to be careful. She was somewhat relieved not only for the finances, but also because, much as she hated him right now, she didn't like conflict and wanted still to be sociable and, if she could, in time, get used to the idea of the tart. At least until all this mess was sorted out.

Chapter 6

This next week, Stella decided, was going to be both interesting and different. Firstly, she had a job to get ready for. She needed to work out her new routine so that she could fit in her yoga after work, her household chores and so on. She also needed to plan what she was going to wear. Should she ask David how smart or casual she needed to be? She would think about that. Secondly, the Bury society ladies thought she had a new man in tow. What to do about that? There would be more questions from them for sure. Should she keep up the pretence and let them make the rest up as they go along or should she put them out of their misery? Tough choice.

It had been so long since Stella last had paid employment. How would she cope with the new technology? Sure, she knew how a laptop worked and could send an email, but things had moved on, hell in her day computers were stand-alone, not much networking and the internet was a dial up modem affair. Now things were so fast at home with fibre broadband and 4G, what was the office system going to be like? This worried her. In addition, although she knew she had been exceptionally good at her old job, now she was rusty, and could she pick it all up again? This wasn't like Stella to worry. Normally she was a confident woman, but the goal posts were moving.

Given the way Tony was yesterday, Stella decided whatever happened, it was over. So, she spent Monday morning contacting the utility companies and the local council to get all the bills transferred into her own name. It was mostly straightforward once you got past digital Doris and managed to speak to a human being in the right department. She even managed to get some of the accounts switched to better tariffs, ha, she felt smug. Now she could do a proper spreadsheet to keep track of her income and outgoings to make sure she was surviving.

After an energy bursting salad, with lime and peanut-dressing, her hunger pangs were gone. She decided to ring David, she didn't want to over or under dress for next Monday. Stella walked into the lounge, sat down, and dialled. He answered.

"Hi David, it's Stella, sorry to ring you at work—" Before she could go any further David interrupted, "Stella, please don't say you have changed your mind. I've been thinking about this new venture while I was relaxing yesterday between cases I was preparing. I'm excited about you starting. I think it will be great for both of us."

"No, no David, I haven't changed my mind. I won't lie, I am terrified that I'll let you, and me, down, but I need to give it a go, if only to work off your fee. I don't want to start off on the wrong foot by not looking the part, too smart or too casual. Does that make sense?"

"Oh, is that all," he chuckled. "Well, I wouldn't do jeans, and a ball gown is probably over the top, but a sensible skirt and blouse or jumper will be just fine. Fishnets and four-inch patent leather shoes is probably going to increase the office footfall once word gets out but given my clients, you won't appreciate that one bit. Has that helped?"

"Yes David, tremendously. Thank you. What time do you want me in on Monday?"

"About 9ish is fine, and there is plenty of parking outside the office. See you then."

"Yes, see you then."

Stella was glad she called, at least she had got that out of the way. She put the phone down and sat back in the chair. She felt more relaxed about this already. David had a strange way of putting her at her ease, a way that she liked.

Feeling positive now and energised from lunch, she checked her *Mind Body* app on her phone. There was a hot yoga class starting in an hour. Perfect, she thought, I can get some energy burned off today. Must not get lazy. Now she was working she would need to exercise to avoid losing fitness from sitting in the office. A realisation, she would be sitting, in an office, Monday to Friday, nine 'til five. She laughed out loud. Oh my god, Stella her own bread winner!

She bounded up the stairs and got herself ready in record time, she was off to the Self Centre, strangely just around the corner from David's office, maybe she could do some yoga at lunchtime, or join Unit 1, a local and respected independent gym, for a cardio session. That decision would have to wait. She walked in, still full of energy almost bouncing with newfound enthusiasm. Carol was there, teaching for Sam who usually took hot yoga, and so was Trudy. They both saw the way she bounced came in and Carol said, "Well, good to see you so full of beans today."

Trudy said, "I think I can guess why. New man and a spring in her step. Who's a lucky girl then?"

"Hey, Trudy, you are so far off the mark, but I'll let you think what you like and not tell you anything to dispel those wonderful rumours that you ladies are spreading. Almost excommunicated, but still the centre of your gossip factory, I love it." Stella thought as she beamed ear to ear and told Carol, "Get that heat up and let's gets those buns and abs burning. I'm ready for a good

session." Stella placed her mat in the middle of the class, water bottle and towel within reach and was ready to go at it.

By the end of the workout, an hour of fast-paced bending, stretching and planks all in 30-degree heat, the whole class were drenched, but Stella was absolutely buzzing with it. Trudy collared her, "Fancy a pick me up juice at Ice after a quick shower?"

"Yeah, why not?" replied Stella.

They sat at the table and waited for their fresh juices to arrive, Stella – apple and elderflower, Trudy – orange and clementine. They sat opposite and Stella looked around. No one else she knew there, which was surprising as this was the latest in place to be seen. Its rustic warehouse décor and old tables gave it an ambience that outweighed the slow service. Stella didn't have to wait long until Trudy broached the subject of her supposed new man.

"So, this dishy, suave, well dressed David chap from Nero on Saturday morning. You kept him a secret. How long, and give me all the details. Judging by what I heard you've done very well. Although I thought you might take a bit longer to get over Tony, you know proper mourning type of time."

Stella chose to ignore the last snipe. "David is a solicitor, he is charming, he took me to dinner at the Angel on Saturday night and that's all you are getting from me. As for waiting, given the way Fuckwit behaved, who could blame me?" No lies there, but lots of misinformation to be wrongly deduced.

"Given the way you came into yoga today, that's not all you're getting from him though." Trudy was desperate to be the first to know, and this information would get her well up the society pecking order.

Stella lowered her eyes to the table pretending to be coy and told Trudy, "You are getting no more information from me to take back to those gossip mongers you mix with. The only thing I will tell you, is that I will be seeing a lot more of David, and I can't wait." That should do it. The drinks had arrived, and both had downed half in one gulp to quench their thirsts after yoga.

Trudy couldn't down her second half quickly enough and made excuses, virtually running from the Ice café in order to earn her brownie points with the society. Stella sat calmly, steadily. She enjoyed that misinformation session and was going to enjoy the rest of her juice in her own time.

She must have sat there on her own a full half hour letting her mind wander from her former life to where she is now and going forward, cleansing her life from the society and her arrogant, cheating, controlling husband, her new job, and David. She thought about him and curiously she felt a warmth stirring inside. Yes, she decided he was a nice-looking and good-hearted man, and she enjoyed his company. She smiled.

Stella arrived home and poured herself another protein rich smoothie, ready-made from the fridge. She went outside and sat on the patio watching the late afternoon turn towards evening. She enjoyed the tranquillity of her back garden. She was not overlooked and, although there were roads and traffic nearby, most of it was light and didn't detract from some relaxation. She enjoyed this time of day. In a former life this was the time when dinner had been prepared and she could unwind for an hour before Tony came home. Stella loved to listen and smell nature all around. Dragonflies hovered around the pond, bees scurried from flower to flower collecting their beloved nectar, and a host of birds, depending on the season, could be seen going about their daily lives. At this time of day many birds were thinking about going back to their homes, nests or roosts for the evening. Others were swooping and diving all about trying to catch a meal of gnat or fly. It was peaceful – almost meditative to her. She sat facing the pond her feet up on a chair, gently cupping her glass while the rest of the world rushed about in its own madness. This time was her sanctuary time. For over an hour she sat in total silence, no one speaking, and enjoyed every moment of the solitude. It was the first time since he left that she had felt able to do this and although her body was full of energy, her mind was still watching and absorbing the real beauty of nature.

Once her smoothie was gone and a while after that, Stella got up and went inside. The evening was spent making herself an omelette and taking another shower before climbing into bed to watch the olds. Stella had called the news that for years, simply because it was never new, more a repeat of the previous day's hashed stories.

Tuesday and Wednesday passed by without anything really happening. Popping to the shops for bits 'n' bobs and keeping on top of the housework. She managed to book an appointment, although she was not quite sure how, to have her hair done on Saturday. Normally she would need to wait weeks if not months for a Saturday slot, but Darren the only Vidal Sassoon trained hairdresser in Bury had a cancellation. Poor old Mrs Bambury, such a shame dying like that, but she was a good age. Stella didn't mind stepping into a dead lady's chair, not for a Saturday cut anyhow.

The post on Thursday came as usual at eleven-thirty a.m., but this time there was a letter for her that she wasn't expecting. It was franked from Irwin Mitchell, a firm of solicitors in Cambridge. She opened it and could barely believe what she was reading.

'We act for Mr Anthony Green and are instructed that sadly

the marriage between you has drawn to an end.

Mr Green would wish us to try and resolve the issues now caused as amicably as possible to obtain a clean break resolution.

Mr Green proposes a divorce based upon your unreasonable behaviour leading to the irretrievable breakdown of the marriage. He would not seek costs against you for this.

He also instructs us that you have reached a settlement regarding finances, in that you will keep the house, mortgage free and our client will keep all his investments. He will pay you £1000 per month until Brian finishes his first degree. Thereafter, there will be a clean break between you. Each of you will retain your cars and any other assets you may have, and our client will make no claim against the Trust Fund.

We would invite you to seek independent legal advice with regards to this matter but confirm that our client will not be responsible for your legal costs.

Yours'

Her jaw fell open and she threw the letter down in a rage, missing the table and landing face down on the carpet. My unreasonable behaviour, the bloody cheek, the bastard. I suppose I made him leave for that tart of a PA he has been shagging behind my back. He won't seek costs! COSTS! I'll give him costs. Clean break – in his neck! He was having a laugh. No, I will not seek legal advice, they can deal with this. Stella sat for ten minutes furious at what she had read. Once she was a little calmer, she picked it up from the carpet and read it again. With determination she stormed to the study.

Stella opened her laptop and typed:

'Dear Sirs,

Thank you for your letter which is, frankly, a one-sided piece of fiction and garbage.

I have no need to see a solicitor and will defend this myself should your client be foolish enough to take on an angry former wife with a brain. The divorce, if issued will be contested, no doubt racking up your precious costs, but not mine. The marriage failed because your client decided he would like to shag a younger model, a bimbo who flatters him for his money. I called that his unreasonable behaviour, not mine. It is also his adultery, if you know anything about the law, which I imagine that you do. If and when this is settled, I will divorce him, the pleasure of paying for it will be his and on the basis of his adultery.

As for the finances, your client came into my home last week and tried to bully me into accepting this pathetic and feeble attempt at an offer. I threw him out and told him it was not acceptable. He later text to apologise and confirmed he would pay me the said £1000 per month. I have the text. More unreasonable behaviour from him. This too will be contested at great expense to your client if that is what he wants. He could, of course, become a reasonable human being and suggest a decent and fair settlement for the last twenty-five years of my almost totally wasted life, cleaning up after him and looking after the house at the expense of my own career. You may like to give him some advice yourselves.

Once all that is agreed, we can then progress this smoothly and, sadly for you, relatively inexpensively. It is your client's choice.

Yours'

She marched straight to the post office and posted it. Let him chew on that, the bastard. How dare he? She hoped it would get to him on Friday and ruin his weekend.

Once home, she changed into her fitness gear. She needed to

vent her anger, and the best place for it was at Unit 1. She drove there barely noticing the traffic and only by luck the old lady crossing the road from behind the parked car by the shop. Stella went straight on the bike for twenty minutes, peddling frantically the whole time. Then she did some heavy ball work for another ten. Each time she threw the ball at the wall, it was going straight at Tony's head. Still angry, she went for the ropes; two inch-and-a-half thick pieces of rope to pound and swing for as long as she could. She pummelled those ropes into the ground, each one on Tony's arse or back. Exhausted, but still angry, she picked up some gloves and went upstairs to the mat area. Here she punched the punch bag hard and fast. Tony's kidneys, head, chest and balls would not survive that. She went into the shower turned it on and sat behind the curtain and sobbed.

When she had calmed down enough, she left the gym and called Julie. Julie was her best friend, and although they didn't speak much, whenever the other was needed it was a given that they would move heaven and earth to help each other out.

They met at Woodbridge School and became lifelong friends, both sharing the same sense of humour and both caring deeply for each other, looking out for one another at every turn. As time went on, they saw less and less of each other. They developed their own lives and families but always kept in touch and saw each other a couple of times a year to catch up. Julie was proud to be asked to be Brian's godmother and enjoyed seeing him develop into the fine young man that he is. Stella was there when Julie's first marriage collapsed within two years. Julie could take the beatings no more and eventually turned to Stella in shame and failure. Stella took her in for a month until she secured her own place and was able to start to rebuild her shattered self-esteem and confidence. That took several years, but now Julie was as strong as ever, loving a real man of a husband and a stunning daughter, now eight years old, and every bit her mother's child.

"Julie, I need to see you, now." Julie would know from Stella's tone that this was something serious but didn't know what and so she told Stella she would be at hers in an hour.

As soon as Julie arrived Stella hugged her and cried some more. Her whole body weight being held by the arms around Julies neck. She thought she had no more tears, but they came anyway. Julie said nothing and hugged her back – tight. An, I am not letting go hug, with her hands stroking her back to comfort her.

After several minutes the hug broke, Julie gently settled Stella on the sofa and said, "Right, I will get us both a large glass of white." Julie knew where both it and the glasses were, and Stella was happy to let Julie pour.

She sat down and handed Stella her glass. Stella's hand shook as she took the glass and placed it to her lips. They both took a long mouthful and eventually Julie said, "OK Stella, this must be serious, what do you want to tell me?"

Over the course of the next half an hour, Stella told Julie all about Tony, the affair, throwing him out, the drink-driving charge, the society desperate for gossip, Tony coming round, the financial issues, the revenge holiday booking, the solicitor's letter, her response. Stella held back from telling Julie about David and the new job. This conversation was all about her problems and not her future. Julie appeared stunned by all of this; thirty years thrown away for a younger bit of stuff. Julie sat and listened, her hand in Stella's, then an arm around the shoulders and tissues always at the ready to catch each tear as it fell.

"Three questions Stella. How are you coping? How is Brian?

And why the fuck didn't you tell me this weeks ago?"

Stella replied, "I'm mostly doing OK. I get on with my daily life all right, it's when he doesn't come home after work that it's toughest, by bedtime I am used to him not being there now. Brian is the rock you would expect him to be. He's offered several times to come home, but I always say no. His studies are far too important for him right now. I'm not sure what he thinks of his father right now, but that's between them to sort out. I didn't tell you for the same reason you never told me about the beatings. Shame, embarrassment, hoping it would sort itself out and we could get back to normal without anyone having to find out. It was the solicitor's letter that made me realise it's over. It really brought my anger to the fore. It made me realise that the last thirty years are over, and I don't want him back, not even if he begged. I need to make myself a new life."

They talked and talked. Before she realised it, Julie had had a second large glass of wine. She poured a third for herself. Still in the kitchen, she called her husband and explained the crisis. He was, of course, fine with it and said that he could look after their daughter without any problem, and he would see her tomorrow. That was that then. "Stella, I am not going to drive tonight as I have had too much to drink. Sorry girl, but you are stuck with me! We can talk all night if we have to."

Stella looked up at Julie, smiled and felt very relieved she would not be alone.

"Julie, you are a marvel. I'm so glad to have you in my life, I don't know what I would've done without you coming round today. Thank you."

They were now starting to get tipsy and Julie asked, "Is Pizza Town still there and do they still deliver?"

It was used occasionally for a Friday night treat and film on the sofa. A beer and pizza night they called it. "Yes, great idea."

So that was sorted. Pizza ordered and wine, not beer, the evening was set.

The pizza was delivered and enjoyed by them both over discussions about the situation. Sitting either end of the sofa without any background noise and being careful not to drop pizza on the carpet. Conversation soon became general chat about the old days, things they got up to in school, life in general. The two of them, now very tipsy, giggled to each other at some of the tales. They even touched on the disaster that is Brexit and wondered if it would ever end and how much money had been wasted on it so far.

They put Netflix on and Bridget Jones to provide background, a great chick flick to chill with. They compared Hugh Grant's character to Tony and decided the character possibly had slightly more morals than the errant soon to be ex-husband. Stella told Julie about David and how it could be a new beginning. Julie decided that this David chap could be worth pursuing and who knows, it may work between them.

Stella laughed it off, but the seeds sown in the pit of her stomach by those butterflies were starting to sprout. Stella secretly hoped she wouldn't cock this up. By the time the film finished, they were both more than a little pissed and ready for bed. Julie went to the spare room and Stella took her in some fresh towels and said goodnight before falling into her own bed and a deep drunken sleep.

Chapter 7

When Stella woke, her head was pounding. She lay, bleary eyed, trying to focus on the ceiling, hearing the birdsong outside coming in through the open window. What had she done last night? Whatever it was, she hoped she wasn't in trouble. Then she remembered, Julie. *'Oh God, I hope she's OK and not feeling as bad as I am.'*

Stella got up and crept downstairs. She poured herself a large glass of fresh orange, well, as fresh as the carton made it. She took an ibuprofen, put some coffee on, and sat by the breakfast bar. It was a hard job to stop her head from dropping to the countertop. It wasn't long before Julie came down.

"I hope I don't look as bad as you," Stella said as she poured Julie an orange and proffered a pain killer.

"I hope you feel worse," laughed Julie.

Neither had had a girlie night like that for a long time, they were out of practice. It was though, just what they needed. Bonds reformed, and Stella got loads off her chest.

"Sorry you feel like you do, but I really needed that to get things in perspective. You really helped me last night and I am sure once my head recovers, I'll be able to move on properly. Thanks, Julie." Stella reached out and softly squeezed Julie's hand.

Julie responded, "Shit, I feel like such a lightweight these days, but I had a great time. Glad to be of help. We must try to get together more often to keep each other in the loop and get more practice at this, otherwise, the next time will kill us, and we'll be grateful for it! Are you up to a light breakfast? I can rustle something up from your fridge in about an hour once the blood decides it's safe to venture into my brain again."

They sat for a while nursing sore heads and hoping that their respective brains would soon kick in. Little chat, the odd smile at the results of the previous night. Stella moved first and went for the shower. The water from the rainfall shower head soothing away the dimness of her brain bringing it back towards normality. Julie followed a few minutes behind. They both arrived back in the kitchen at about the same time, and, as promised, Julie hit the fridge to see what was there to knock up a hangover-cure of a power breakfast. She managed to come up with a strange concoction of oats, coconut and matcha powder with some maple syrup. Looked god awful but gave them the boost they need – and fast.

They decided that neither was going anywhere anytime soon, so they sat and talked. Once more in their regular places on the sofa, both with their feet on the seat and knees drawn up to their chests. Stella explained to Julie the circumstances of how she got a new job. Stella was still nervous about it, but when they broke it down, how hard could it be? Everything that she would need to do, Stella knew and had done and could do more. Her years of experience at the landscape architects had set her in good stead and it wasn't like rocket science. Julie was such a pick me up and by the end of the conversation Stella's confidence about the job was increasing and her nerves were dissipating.

It was lunchtime before Julie decided it was safe enough to drive. They said their goodbyes, keep in touches and went on their respective ways. A final tight hug on the doorstep. Stella watched as Julie pulled back off the drive and returned the wave as she pulled away before gently closing the door. Stella decided to spend the afternoon in Cambridge getting herself some stationery for her new job on Monday. She parked at the park and ride in Newmarket road and caught the bus into the city. The route was mundane but sitting on the bus enabled Stella to watch the shoppers wandering about, or the dog walkers on their way to the park. The hustle and bustle of Cambridge was certainly greater than Bury. It dropped her two minutes from Lion Yard shops, which had her favourite John Lewis in there. She made a beeline for it and chose a variety of stationery supplies: Post-it's in pink and a new calculator. She treated herself to a Cross pen and pencil, and other items she thought may come in handy, including a notebook for her to take notes of what David wanted her to do and how he wanted it done. She bought a sandwich in M&S and then had her nails done at the nearest nail bar. A simple French polish but it made her feel good to be even a little pampered. She watched the speedy and skilful way the technicians worked their magic on her nails. That, apart from her hair, was Stella ready to return to the working environment on Monday.

Once she was finished, she went home, parked her car, and collected her shopping from the boot. She went to the door. Her hand reached the handle and Stella was concerned. Strange, it wasn't locked. She put her bags down and nervously opened the door, hoping to take the unannounced visitor by surprise. Putting her head gingerly inside to see what was happening, she stopped dead. Hang on, there's music playing. David Grey. That can only be one person. Stella picked up her shopping and rushed in shouting, "Brian, Brian, where are you?"

Brian appeared at the top of the stairs, bounded down them and took his mother into his arms. It was a deep meaningful hug that can only be shared between mother and son.

"I have missed you my darling boy, what are you doing here and where is your car?"

Brian let his mother go and looked deep into her eyes, "I've come to see you, two months is too long, and it seems you needed to see me. I'm beyond up to date at uni, so I thought a long weekend was in order. The car, if you had bothered to look, is in the garage because I wanted to surprise you, as you weren't here when I got home. Now who's for a drink and a chat?"

"Oh, come on, let's get into the kitchen and sit down. I'll pour you a glass, red or white? A quick one, then I'm taking you to The Griffin."

"A small red, please. It's not The Griffin, hasn't been for years. You know it's changed hands several times since grandad died. It's now The Cadogan Arms."

Stella would never accept that. "Brian, it was The Griffin when I grew up and we went there regularly on a Sunday for Grandad to play darts, and it will be The Griffin 'til I die. It's the family pub and always will be. Sure, Dave has changed it a lot and it now does really great food, but it's still the Griffin. Always was and always will be."

"Ok, Mum, whatever," Brian sighed. He would never change his mother's mind on that. Even after his grandfather died, Mum and Dad still went for years every Sunday to see the old boys playing darts and to catch up. Once it was modernised that all stopped, progress they called it. The pub became far more of a food outlet, and families travelled to meet and eat, and it made more profit. The regulars, however, saw it differently, it was no longer the village pub. That died and, although they sometimes popped in for a pint, it was never the same. Even though the smoking had gone, the place remained nicotine-stained walls and smoke stinking fabrics on the seats where the old boys sat. They chose the same seat every week and played their darts for beer, talking about the racing, football, and the latest crop information. Change happened but was this was true progress – it broke communities up. As an aspiring GP, Stella believed, he would feel that was a mistake within the modern society.

They sat at the breakfast bar and drank their wine. Stella could see that Brian had already raided the fridge as, as usual, his dishes and cutlery were placed neatly by the sink. Why he couldn't make the extra step to find the dishwasher amazed Stella, but he was her boy and it didn't matter. Stella told Brian she would change his bed sheets since Julie had slept in them last night.

"That's no problem, Mum, if it was only one night. It's not as though she smells. How is she?"

Stella told him about the catch-up news from last night, and that Julie was fine apart from her sore head this morning. Brian found that amusing. He had grown up with Mum and Julie and knew what they were like when they got together, but rarely did it end up with sore heads, they must be getting old he chuckled to himself. Then Stella drove Brian to the Griffin. It was only a ten-minute drive, but very pleasant going through a couple of Suffolk villages and passed many fields with their crops of beet or rape growing nicely. You would always see pheasant playing 'chicken' on the roads and the odd sparrow hawk seeking lunch near the verges.

They found a table in the rear on the deck, overlooking the grass. Quieter than inside, and little road noise from passing traffic. Both liked to be away from all the noise of other diners, and they did cram them in there. Brian settled on pie with bacon chop, ham hock and onion, with a serving of mash. Stella went for the fish: pan-fried sea trout with monkfish cheeks. As always, the food was well cooked and the staff attentive. They continued to reminisce about days gone by and how wonderful Brian's childhood had been. With the pleasant sunny weather and only a light breeze to move the leaves on the trees, the whole process of lunch became a joy. Brian confirmed he still wanted to return to Suffolk after he qualified and practice as a GP. Yes, the hours were long and the pay poor compared to other areas of medicine, but he felt strongly about community and how the elderly in particular were getting a bum deal with modernisation of society as a whole. He would do what he could to restore that balance, albeit only in a small way.

After dining they returned to home and poured more red, *Killer Roo* from Australia, a fantastic full-bodied and intensely chocolate flavoured Shiraz – it was rather special. Brian asked what had been going on over the last few weeks – really going on. Stella took in the aroma of the wine as she raised the round bowl to her lips, its heady hints encouraging her to savour it. Stella was in no mood to recount everything for the second night in a row and told him they would talk about it tomorrow. There was nothing that Brian could do to change that and so he let it lie until the morning.

Since Brian was home, Stella decided to do him a full breakfast: juice, cereal, toast, bacon, sausage, mushrooms, and egg. It was really good to see him, and she would spoil him while he was there. It was all ready and in the warming drawer before Brian came downstairs. There was no way he would miss the wafting bacon flavour enticing him into the kitchen. Stella smiled as he walked in and they both sat at the breakfast bar to enjoy the meal. It was served on warm plates and with a serving of gratitude and a kiss to his forehead. After breakfast was finished,

Stella told Brian she was going to the hairdressers but would be back about one, so he could keep himself company 'til then. Stella could tell that Brian was not best pleased with his mother but he would simply have to wait until she was ready to tell him. She would tell him, but not in a rush, and when they had the time to do it properly. As Stella left the house, she saw Brian simply shrug his shoulders.

When Stella got home Brian told her that her hair looked lovely. She knew he was only placating her and that he really just wanted to know what was happening.

"Right Mum, let's sit down in the lounge and you can tell me what's really been going on between you and Dad." Brian got them both a glass of wine.

Stella sat in the chair and looked at her son. Her face was sad as this was the telling of the hidden parts of the marriage. The bits no child should find out. With sadness in her voice, eyes and heart she began, "Your dad was always good-looking and charming. The ladies loved him, and he loved the attention. I was over the moon when we got together. For me it was for life. I was working as a landscape architect and Dad was just starting in his own career. When you came along, I gave up work and devoted my life to both of you. I kept house, and he provided the money, standard post-wedding stuff really. We were happy, well, at least I was. Dad was made a director and we had that huge party in the garden, do you remember? Nothing could go wrong, we were the perfect couple in my eyes, and our friends' too. With the new job came longer hours and more responsibility. He needed a PA to look after him, keep his diary that sort of thing. First it was Alison. She lasted a couple of years but had a child. That's when the new bit came along. Sue, he called her, Tart is my name." Stella swallowed hard at the mention of her. "Young airhead, blonde, single mum, got the exams but no ability he said. He didn't mention the legs, the baby-blue eyes or the firm pert breasts though. I was fed up waiting for him to come home every night from Cambridge and it was getting later and later. We rowed about it, just his job he said, he needed to do the hours to keep our lifestyle going. I would have the odd drink and go to bed, leave him to fend for himself when he came in.

Anyway, one Friday night a few weeks ago we were supposed to be going to the Apex to see a live band, some Eagles tribute band, supposed to be OK. He called to say he was going to be late. When he got back I'd had several glasses of wine, I know I shouldn't. We had a humdinger of a row. He was in the shower and a text came through from his tart, I will spare you the details, but I saw it and I knew." A tear escaped from Stella's eye and rolled gently down her cheek. "It was quite brutal, and your dad just blurted out that he was having an affair with Sue. I had driven him to it with all the drinking and rowing, and I was never awake when he came home. I don't think that he meant for it to come out, but the writing was staring him in the face, and he couldn't deny it. He looked at me, horrified, and I stopped dead for a few seconds letting this confession sink in. Then I lost it even more. I called him some dreadful, but deserved, things and kicked him square in the nuts. I told him he had five minutes to pack and go before he got a second kick. He didn't wait for that and was gone.

I was deeply hurt and upset by this. I expected him to come crawling back. I don't know if I would have taken him back, but he could've tried. Thing is, he didn't and that hurt even more. I missed him in bed, and I missed knowing he was coming home. One night, I was especially upset, no real reason, it hit me hard, and I had too much to drink. The next day I was on my way to yoga when I got stopped, over the limit. Court was traumatic, but this solicitor David Hughes helped me. It made the papers and your nan found out."

Stella took a mouthful of wine and continued. "Then your dad, and it got even sillier. Two days ago, I got a letter from his lawyer, he wants a divorce. My solicitor has offered me a job to assist him, and I've taken it. No idea what I'll be doing, but it brings me in some money and will take my mind off all the other problems going on."

She paused once more and took in a deep breath. "There, there you have it all now, Brian. I'm trying to keep it together and really didn't want you fretting about me, but now you know it all and I know you would have only gone on until I told you. Things will be OK though, I'm sure of that. Financially we have the trust fund, and that will go a long way.

Oh, I almost forgot, when dad told me he was cancelling the credit card I booked myself on a safari. I'm looking forward to that one. Wish I'd seen his face when he checked his bank and that came up."

Brian sat patiently listening to every word and let his mum finish. He got up and sat next to his mother. He put his arms around her, pulled her head to his shoulder and hugged her tight.

"Mum, I will always be here for you, no matter what. If you get back together fine, if you don't, still fine, I'll support you in your decisions. As for me, now I know the full story I want to go and break his arms. I want nothing more to do with him or his arrogant family. They always thought they were better than everyone else."

"You are angry Brian I understand that, but much as it pains me right now, he is your dad. I will not stop you, whatever you want to do with him."

They talked around the houses for several hours before Brian went to get them both pizza. Stella knew she only had one the other day, but what the hell. The next day Brian had to go back to Edinburgh. They spent the rest of the evening discussing Brian and his college work. This was a much better topic of conversation and the mood was easy and light. It made them both feel far happier. He was doing really well, and some professors were already requesting him for their courses next year. Just like his dad, he was popular and well regarded by everyone.

The next morning Brian left for the drive back to college. As he left Stella had a tear in her eye. When he pulled away it crept to her cheek and she sighed as she used the back of her hand to wipe it away. Her eyes didn't leave the car until it could be seen no more. Stella remained on the doorstep listening to the engine and within a minute even that could not be heard. She went back inside and sprang into action. *"Oh my god, I start work tomorrow and I haven't even got the shopping in or tidied the house this weekend!"* She rushed round the house like a rocket, usual routine with the added extra of stripping Brian's bed and changing the sheets. Sainsbury's was thankfully quiet and Stella got her usual groceries, but also some extra bits so she could make herself packed lunches for work. Other than Sainsbury's, there were no shops near the office, and that was a fifteen-minute walk round the streets. She popped into Curry's and bought herself a smoothie maker. She'd always wanted one but could never quite justify it to herself. Now she had that justification. It would provide some great energy-packed drinks for her at work.

Stella got home and unpacked everything. She poured a glass of wine and set about reading the smoothie book and the recipes. Sitting in the lounge, the words and pictures made her feel hungry and she toyed with the idea of getting something to eat. *'No time like the present'*, and so Stella made and thoroughly enjoyed her first smoothie from the machine. She went upstairs and spent an hour going through various outfits to wear in the morning. She settled on a white silk blouse with a navy pencil skirt. That would be a safe bet she thought. She would gauge it to dress up or down for Tuesday once she got there.

Now, time to relax. She drew the bath, added salts and bubbles, and clambered in for a soak. "Alexa, play me some light jazz." She had earned it this week. Why was it all so complicated? She took the razor and tidied everything up. Tonight, she really loved the bath: hot, relaxing bubbles and the bath salts. She lay back and let the music from the speaker wash over her, through her, down to her soul. At this moment, she knew she would be fine.

Chapter 8

The night was terrible. Could Stella sleep? Why not? It was two a.m. and Stella was wide awake. *"Try to sleep or you will look crap in the morning."* It was no good, all she could think about was the morning, the new job. Why was she so nervous? He wasn't going to kill her. He wanted to help. Oh, for God's sake, this is no good at all.

Three a.m. – now it's only three a.m. – only another four hours 'til it's time to get up. Come on Stella, sleep lady, sleep. She rolled over to her left side and pulled the pillow down. Nope, no good. Over onto the right, same problem. *"Nerves are going to ruin this; I will be laughed at completely. What will he think of me?"* Onto her back watching the ceiling, the shadow from the ceiling light. No use, just no use. Stella drifted for a while.

Half past five, that's it, there is no point now in going back to sleep at all. Even if I did, I would be late for work and that would be worse than a puffy eyed zombie. Coffee, strong to wake me up. Stella got up and went downstairs, shuffled into the kitchen, and put the kettle on. She turned on the news channel, more Brexit, at this time of the morning, does it never end? She perched herself at the breakfast bar and half-awake, drank the coffee, it woke her a little. Her head and shoulders remained hunched and her eyes only half open. A long shower, that's what she needed. Back upstairs and into the shower, hot and revitalising, it was doing the trick. Stella stayed in there for a long time washing and rinsing her hair, feeling the water from the shower rain down her back and legs, then arching her back to let the water flow to the front. Now she felt awake.

    Stella returned to the kitchen and made her breakfast, simple boiled egg and toast. She also made a banana and peanut butter smoothie, adding in coffee as she felt she would need that later. Some fruit, crackers, chopped tomato, cucumber and carrot sticks for lunch. She returned upstairs and sat by the dressing table, seven a.m. and she still had plenty of time. She looked at herself in the mirror, this was it. This was day one of the rest of her life, a new job and a new start. The drive to the office, the new office, less than ten minutes away. My god her eyes still looked dreadful, but she was a master at the makeup and a concealer connoisseur. She took her time, she wanted to look as natural as possible, not like these kids today with the painted-black, thick eyebrows, but simple and subtle. She achieved it. Looking at herself afterwards she was happy with the transformation from twenty minutes ago. Thank you, God, she thought quietly to herself. She finished getting ready in the clothes she had picked out for herself last evening and put a simple necklace on with a pendant in the shape of a heart, iridescent colours highlighting it. A final look in the mirror, yes that was as good as it was going to get this morning.

    Stella headed downstairs for the last time that day and got her bag of new office supplies together. She still had half an hour to kill, so she poured some fresh juice and watched some more olds. Why don't they shoot that heckler outside Westminster? Every morning he bawls the same indistinguishable monologue. He frustrated her. Right, that's it, no more stalling, or pacing the rooms to be done. Let's do this. Let's become a worker bee.

    Once in her car, Stella checked her face in the rear-view mirror before putting on the seatbelt and nervously she drove the short distance to David's office. Through the back roads to where

Moreton Hall was ever expanding, threatening to link Thurston with Bury St Edmunds, (she thought this would be a tragedy for the village) and down past the new school, built for the ever-increasing estate. As she turned off the roundabout at John Banks Honda garage, she became nervous again. This was it, two minutes away and there was no going back now. She pulled into the parking space at 8.55 a.m., perfect, not too early and definitely not late. Stella got out of the car and collected her bits, she stood and looked at her new home for the weekdays. The estate was built in the '80s, primarily as light industrial units, but over the years had changed use to encompass gyms, health studios, micro-brewers and specialist food outlets. David had taken on one of the smaller units. From the outside there was parking for about eight cars and a half-glazed wall with a door to the left-hand side. On the widow it stated boldly 'David Hughes, Criminal Defence Solicitor'. *"Well, no need to stand there gawping,"* she said to herself. She lifted her head and strode purposefully in through the door. An electric bell sounded announcing her presence.

She expected to see a solicitor's reception like any other, chairs, plants, reception desk and people scurrying behind it, perhaps a coffee machine. Nope, that was not this office. Instead, she had walked into a wide corridor with a few formal interview seats against one wall, fabric-covered and slightly worn. Further down, were two painted, white doors on the left-hand side. Down the right-hand side were two offices, both with windows facing into the corridor. From the first door David appeared. He was wearing jeans and brogues, a shirt and a pale pink Pringle jumper. Stella felt decidedly over-dressed!

With a firm handshake and a warm smile, David greeted Stella, "Hey, Stella, you found it then? I'm delighted to see you.

Welcome to my world, small though it is. Let me show you round the place."

Where was David's suit, all solicitors wore suits to work don't they? David took Stella to the first door on the left and went in. Stella followed. "The most important room," he announced. It was the kitchen. A kettle, sink and a few cupboards both underneath and at eye level. There was a fridge and a microwave. "Can I get you a drink? Tea, coffee?"

"Thanks David, a coffee would be great."

Wow, a boss that makes the coffee, for a moment she thought she was being appointed tea monitor.

While the kettle was boiling, David took her round the rest of his kingdom, not that it took that long. The other door was the toilets, a male and female one. "Strictly for the staff, in time you'll understand why." The office furthest from the door was next. This was Stella's office, she hadn't been expecting her own office! The last place she'd worked it was open-plan with everyone in together, and Stella thought she would be at the reception desk. It was a good size for one, her own desk and a computer, telephone, shelves (almost empty) to the side, a printer behind that and a couple of filing cabinets. The chair was high backed and executive looking. There was also a window to the rear with a view to other parts of the site, probably the back of Matalan. There were also many individual files, sitting in, what appeared to be, random piles all around the room, yellow, red and blue. It was a mess, and Stella could not work in that. David's room was the same size as Stella's and similar in configuration. His chair was much better though, leather this time. The desk was bigger and, as well as a bookshelf with books and lever arch files on it, there were three filing cabinets.

"Take a seat Stella and I'll get the coffee, white no sugar?"

He had remembered from Nero's the previous week, she liked that. "Yes please." Stella sat alone in the room and took it in further, no family pictures, no children, not a single thing on the walls at all. That, she thought, was strange. The desk was neatly laid out, pens and pencil in a row, keyboard straight and several files on the desk in a neat pile, not like in her office. She felt as though she was about to be interviewed, sitting with her back straight hands resting on the thighs, fingers clasped together.

David returned with the coffee and sat in his chair. "There you are."

David went first. "OK Stella, welcome again. This is where it all happens. I am not a bad lawyer, been doing it for years and the courts and police respect me. As I said, my problem is paperwork. I am my accountant's nightmare, and any time I spend here I'm not earning money so my profit goes down. For the last few years, it's become more and more bureaucratic what with the LAA and quality assurance computerising everything, and I'm struggling. If I wasn't so well respected the LAA would have closed me down last year for my paperwork and records. I don't know if I can afford to go down this route, but I'm willing to give it a try with you though and see what happens. If it's not right next year, I'll be closed down for sure."

"Oh my god, that's terrible. Well, I'll do what I can to help, but I'm rusty and don't know anything about the law either."

"Don't worry about that, that's my job. Sure, you need to know the basics but nothing more, I just need organising. I've not got anything else on today, well nothing that can't wait, so I have all day today to get you up and running and, in a position where you can at least make a start. I don't expect miracles and yes there will be lots of questions over the next few days and weeks, but you have to start somewhere, and I think you're smart enough to pick it up, OK?"

With that David started to talk about the job, from the start, people getting arrested and able to call on him to help, or duty solicitors, like Stella did at court. From there if they are charged you can represent them in the magistrate's court. Serious cases end up in the crown court, and he becomes more of an assistant to the barrister he gives the case to. At each of these different stages, as they end, there is the prospect of getting paid. Which is why each type of work has a different coloured file, blue police station, yellow magistrate's court and red for the crown court. David described how each of the different areas of work needed different levels of attention and skills, with different processes involved. He explained how different outcomes can lead to different levels of pay. He touched on Legal Aid, or Public Funding as it now was, the duty solicitor scheme and private clients. All the while Stella took notes but said nothing. She was becoming confused by all the different combinations, and the complexity of it all.

David continued by talking about the income and outgoings of running the place, SMPs (the regular payments from the Legal Aid Authority) and mentioned typical levels for each type of case. The fact that for private work, you don't go near a court unless money is paid in advance, frequently once the job is complete it becomes very difficult to get the money from the client. Finally, the use of professional agents to assist when he was elsewhere. This was more like the work that Stella understood.

"There is an office manual, we must have one for the LAA audit, but it can be changed and I'm sure once you get to grips with things it will need to be updated. It's in hard copy and also on the server in some cloud somewhere or other."

Stella was feeling a bit bewildered by it all, and by now the coffee cups were empty. "Tell you what Stella, now's probably a good time to refill those cups and get you into your office."

With that David took the cups to the kitchen and put the kettle on. Stella followed but then went into her office, HER office! She sat in her chair and looked about. How was she ever going to understand and sort this mess out?

David returned with cups refreshed. He came round to Stella's side of the desk and turned on the computer. It had a log-on code that Stella wrote down. He showed her the case management system briefly. "This," he explained, "is where everything is stored, all the work we do, the bills in and out and all that financial stuff I sounded like I knew about."

He told Stella that he was going to his office, and the door was always open. She could have a look round the computer system, read a few files to try and get her head into the nuts and bolts of what went on. "Oh, if the phone rings, don't worry about it, I'll take it until you get your confidence going." With that he left her alone.

Stella sat motionless except for her head as she once again scanned the bomb site of a room she found herself in. Where to start and what to do with it all? Well, those files must be first, then she can at least have some tidiness about her. The untidiness of this room surprised her as David was so well dressed and his office was immaculate. Out of sight, out of mind she decided. Stella picked up the nearest pile of files and placed them on her desk. *"First, let's get them in order."* Blue, yellow, red, that was it, and the same with the next, adding to her three piles on the desk. *"No more room, right let's start having a look at the private lives of some criminals and what they have been up to."*

She started on the blue files, the police station files, David had said. They were the thinnest. Inside she could see what the police had said happened, the private and confidential discussions David had with his clients and the advice given, followed by the brief interview notes and a letter to the client detailing the outcome. Stella read several files and started to see a pattern to the advice. Most of the time David was telling his clients to say nothing at all to the police. Why? If they had done nothing, say so, and if they had done it, surely they should own up to what they had done, and, from what Stella was reading most of them, seemingly, had done it. So many people doing terrible things, shoplifters, drug dealers, people fighting their partners or in the pub. This was terrible, and worse than that, this was Bury St Edmunds, this sort of thing didn't go on here, not to this scale!

Moving on to the yellow files, now things were a bit thicker, but not much. Each had a bundle of stapled documents from the prosecution setting out the charges and the evidence, some had statements, many didn't. Stella read some of these files thoroughly. Things were a bit better. Many more were admitting their wrongdoing, pleading guilty and being punished by the courts. Some were pleading not-guilty though and from the statements she read, they were wrong. These witnesses were saying they did it, so why not admit it?

David came to her office and knocked on the door. Stella jumped as she was engrossed in the files. "Right Stella, it's lunchtime, my treat for your first day, the Moreton Hall pub, not brilliant but close."

Stella looked at her watch. It was one o'clock and she hadn't done any work, just read files. David wouldn't like that, she thought. They got to the pub, a short drive, and David found them a table. They both ordered a light meal and a drink. David asked,

"How are you getting on?"

Stella replied that she was sorry as all she had done was read files. She was confused. How could he tell people to say no comment when they had clearly been up to no good? And was there really that much crime in her little town? She wasn't sure she could do this job.

He thought for a few moments and then David explained. Firstly, reading the files was all that he expected this morning, she needed to understand a little about the job and what she would be dealing with. "I don't have any problem with you reading the files. It's good to have an understanding of what I am doing. As for the questioning," here David chuckled, "please do question, it's important." He went on to explain, "It's for the police or prosecution to prove the case, not the defendant. If they can't prove it, and often they can't, then in law the client has done no wrong." As for evidence being against them." He then reminded her of her own case and the incorrect previous convictions and possible stolen identity. "Witnesses, as well as defendants, lie and have their own agenda, and sometimes, witnesses don't even turn up at court. It was not his place to judge anyone." He pointed out to her, "just to help them as best he could. As for the crime levels in Bury, they are terrible and we don't have enough police to protect us, my clients know that well and use it to their advantage."

That seemed to make more sense to Stella, and she was beginning to understand. They finished their lunch and returned to the office. Stella continued to sort the files into their respective piles and continued to read the odd one that looked interesting. She had also noticed that several files, especially the police station ones were in relation to the same clients – Bryan Aves and Simon Brown were certainly individuals Stella did not want to meet. They appeared to be a bit of a crime wave in themselves. David had to pop out in the afternoon to go to the police station, but he was back after only an hour. "One of my regulars, needed a chat, left him to the police interview on his own, he knows what to do, he's had enough practice. We can do his case together on the system. Training from start to finish as it were."

David pulled a chair round to sit beside Stella and between the two of them, Ian James's case went on the system, personal details, details of the allegation and what had happened. David showed Stella how to record the time he had spent with the client. It couldn't be billed until the police made a decision as to what to do with him, but David expected him to be charged later that evening and kept in custody for court in the morning. He had already been in the cells most of Monday, as he was arrested the previous night for a pub fight. Just in case he had to go straight to court the next day, David gave Stella a set of keys and the alarm code.

It was four-thirty p.m. and David told Stella to go home. She had worked hard, and for a first day back at work after such a long break, she must be exhausted. Stella thanked him and said she would be back the next day. She left and drove home.

It was strange indeed, driving home to an empty house after a day's work, a new experience and one she had mixed feelings about. As she drove home her mind went over her day, the office mess, the crime levels. She was so engrossed in her thoughts Stella nearly missed the turning at Fishwick corner to be more accurate. She liked the fact she was once again contributing to society, albeit in a small form, but still wanted someone to share it with. She had never been alone in all her adulthood before Tony left. Since she had eaten at lunchtime, she made a light dinner and put it in the oven while she changed out of her work clothes and relaxed in a much-needed bath. She reflected on her day. She was unsure about the morality of the work but understood it as a safety net for the individual against the state and on balance it was a good day that she had enjoyed. She was looking forward to tomorrow. David was right, she was mentally exhausted after her first day and it would be an early night for her.

Chapter 9

Stella arrived at work, as she did yesterday, a few minutes early. Hers was the only car parked outside the office. David did mention he might be going straight to court if that chap was remanded in custody and he had given her the keys and alarm code. She opened up the office and went inside. Feeling a bit like a trespasser being in this place for only the second day and on her own, she nervously went to her office and put on the light. Yes, everything was there and just as it was yesterday when she left it. A lot tidier but still a way to go before she could accept it as her office and the way she wanted it. She crossed the hallway and went into the kitchen. It was spotless, David had clearly cleaned up their coffee cups from yesterday. He seemed a nice person, a nice boss, not one where menial tasks were beneath him.

She made her coffee and returned to her office, sat in her chair and once more contemplated her surroundings. She recalled her discussion with David the previous day regarding the morality of his work and felt more comfortable about it. At nine a.m. her mobile buzzed. A message from David.

'*Morning Stella, as I mentioned yesterday, I'm going to be in court this morning. Hope to be with you by eleven thirty as this shouldn't take too long. Make yourself at home and see you later. I'm assuming that you're still happy to work for me for the time being!*'

She chuckled and replied,

'*Hi David, I worked that out when you weren't at the office.*

Yes I am here and I will do what I can until you get back, Stella.'

The files that were being sorted yesterday into their respective piles were almost completed, so she decided to finish that job. Having read several files yesterday she had gathered a flavour of what it was about, she declined to read many more, just the odd one that caught her eye as maybe interesting. One such file was blue, and in the name of Charlie Franklin. It couldn't be. Should she have a look? The Charlie she knew was Jane's son. Hesitantly, and feeling like a peeping tom she opened the file. She looked at the custody record. Name yep, date of birth about right, address, bloody hell this was Jane's son. What was he in a police station for and why hadn't Jane said anything to the society or to her specifically? This was gossip indeed. OK moving on down the page, arrested three months ago for possession of cannabis. Drugs, Charlie a druggy, that can't be right. She read on, circumstances of arrest – found outside school premises with cannabis in his school bag. She dare not read any more, had she read too much? She put this file to one side to speak with David about her faux pas when he got back.

Once the files were sifted Stella wanted to check on the system which had been billed, paid, or not and which could be filed as completed. It was apparent there was no discernible system that she could ascertain for this from looking at the files themselves, but she didn't want to use the computer without David there to supervise. In the absence of David, Stella tasked herself to do what she knew she could, accounts work. Let's look at what's in place and let's put a system together that works for me. She found a pile of invoices in a tray, mixed in with a pile of bills from David. What a muddle, no, what a disaster. He wasn't lying when he said he needed help. There were a few lever arch files that contained more of the same in an apparently random order also. *"Well, I daren't touch this lot, they must be in some sort of system but not one that I can understand. If I muddle this lot up, it may take forever to fix. Time to refill my coffee."*

She was coming out of the kitchen for the second time, when David walked in. Very smart in his light grey suit, white shirt, purple tie with matching handkerchief in the top pocket and newly cleaned shoes. He also had a lovely smile on his face. "Hi, David, kettles just boiled, want a coffee?"

"Hi Stella, that's the best, well only, offer I've had today, just milk please. How have you been getting on?"

"Can we have a chat once the coffee is made, please?"

"Of course."

Once the coffee was made David came through to Stella's office and sat. "OK, Stella, give me the bad news."

Firstly, Stella confessed about reading some of the file on Charlie Franklin. She knows the family. She was sorry she'd pried. David explained that Bury was a small town and she would read and see several things regarding people she knew. Some defendants, some victims. It was bound to happen. "The thing is though, we are bound by client confidentiality. We cannot discuss these things with anyone outside the office or court unless it is with the client's consent and that's best in writing to cover you in the event of an insurance claim. It'll take a bit of getting used to, but it's OK and you should know what's going on, it's part of your job. If it hadn't been in the Bury Free Press no one would know about your little mishap, would they? On that note I spoke with the prosecutor today, it was James Purdue, the same prosecutor from two weeks ago, and the same prosecutor we'll be with in court tomorrow." Stella had forgotten with everything else that was going on the she was back in court on Wednesday. "Anyhow I got him to update me on your case. It seems that I was right. Your fingerprints don't match the fingerprints held against your name and previous convictions. You and the other Stella Green are two separate individuals. He's satisfied that sloppy policing, although understandable for a simple drink-drive case, has led to this error and will be sympathetic with you in court. That's great news, isn't it?"

Stella was stunned for a moment. "Yes, I mean no, I mean, oh I don't know what I mean. This last week or so has been so busy with everything else going on, I'd almost forgotten about my case. What are we going to do now?"

David told Stella not to worry about it for now, that was his job. What else did she want to talk about? She told him about the clients' files and also about the invoices and bills. David confirmed that after lunch he would spend time with her on both things, and show her where to find the information in the system. As for the filing system, he apologised, it's not great and please change whatever is needed to make it work for you and, by default, me. He said he needed to get some bits done and Stella should take her lunch now and he would see her at about two-ish.

Stella decided to stretch her legs. She had been at her desk virtually all day and that was not going to be good for her. She left the office and had a walk around the estate. There was nothing much to see, just lost of units similar to David's with different cars outside and lorries driving round delivering or collecting. After half an hour she felt less stiff and went back to the office. Stella made David another cup of coffee and she returned to her desk.

A little while had past when David appeared at her door. "Right, let's get to it. Let's give you the tools and confidence to be productive here," he giggled. They sat side by side at Stella's computer with David taking plenty of time to go through the system. Firstly, the client side of things, so Stella could see what had been billed and paid. Then he took her through the ledgers for the invoicing side. David showed Stella how to make ledger postings. He showed her the CDS6, a return to the LAA to claim all police station and magistrate's cases once they were finished.

Their thighs touched together inadvertently, and Stella felt a momentary shock of electricity from her thigh, round the pit of her stomach, and up to her chest. He showed Stella the bank reconciliation and how that worked on the system. Given the way payments were made from the LAA, it added a further step to the normal accountancy practice of double entry book keeping system that was the foundation of all accounts software, but she thought she got that bit. David asked to watch Stella have a go by herself at navigating the software to make sure she understood and could move between the various pages, clients, ledgers and bank accounts that she would need to.

There were times when David's hand reached out to take control of the mouse to point Stella in the right direction and their hands would touch. There it was again, more electricity. Had David felt it to? Was he doing this deliberately? Stella felt flushed and refused to look David in the face just in case she was being a foolish girl about it. He was only showing her how the system worked, after all. It wasn't as though he was squeezing her hand at the same time. Come on Stella, get a grip.

After about an hour of tutoring, David felt Stella had the basics and left her to have a go by herself while he made coffee. How much coffee do people drink in the office these days, two in the morning, one in the afternoon, Stella would be on a caffeine buzz for days at this rate. She must bring in some herbal tea.

Stella decided that she would first deal with the client files as she was desperate to get rid of the biggest source of mess in the room. With each one in turn, she checked the computer. Her piles were further separated into definitely paid, billed and no idea. Police stations followed by magistrate's followed by crown court. That was the easy part. She found an empty drawer in one of the filing cabinets and cleared the other three half-filled drawers onto the floor. These three drawers would be hers, paid files, billed files and unbilled files. That was the start of the filing clear up done and the end of her second day at work.

Stella left the office with a sense of achievement, she had today made a start in her role and could see some results, although the floor was full again with things taken out of the filing cabinet. David came rushing out after her.

"Stella, tomorrow. I decided I'll pick you up from home since you won't be able to drive after court. If I get to you about nine, that gives us plenty of time. Dress as you always do, and all will be fine. Relax tonight and don't worry, we can talk about what's going to happen on the way."

"Uh, OK, David, see you at nine."

With that Stella drove home. Strangely, she had little appetite that evening. Her mind was rushing, flashing between the thought of tomorrow and losing her licence, and to David and the feelings she felt when their thighs touched and their hands brushed on the mouse. What on earth was she thinking? He was her lawyer and her boss, it was against the rules surely. Anyway, she barely knew him. But he was nice, good-looking, pleasant and, as far as Stella knew, single. But he wouldn't want anything to do with her. She may look good for her age, but she was a drink-driver, a client and an employee. He wouldn't be interested in her, it was a business arrangement.

She managed to rustle herself up an omelette before running a bath. Salts and bubbles with a glass of Chenin Blanc and some light classical music. She got in and relaxed. Her mind started to wander. She was back to David and the thought of him was starting to turn her on. What if it were his hands under the bubbles next to her, resting on her stomach?

She closed her eyes. In her mind it was David's hand that moved up, circling her breast and reaching for the already erect nipple. It was his fingers that caused her to sigh with pleasure as they squeezed the tautness firmly between them. It was his other hand stroking her inner thigh, moving upwards soft and determined. It was his that was now gently rubbing her intimately, making her aroused. It was a subtle touch that made her demand more. His hand became more urgent, entering her and taking her to satiation while she lay there, eyes closed and fantasised.

When she opened her eyes, her hand was shaking as she reached for her wine. What had she done? How could she face him now? Her face would give away her dirty thoughts as soon as she looked at him. She was behaving once more like a crazy teenager with a crush, but the crush was there, developing inside her. She lay longer, quite some time, before she could find the courage to leave the bath and with it, her lustful thoughts of David. She watched each one of them drain away as the bath emptied. She sighed once more, but this time with regret, regret that this was all in her head. Stella set the alarm, got into bed, and finished her wine. She turned out the light, pulled the duvet around her and rolled over. She would dream tonight. She would remember but never divulge that dream.

Stella didn't need the alarm the next morning and as usual she was up in good time. She breakfasted and readied herself for the arrival of the boss, chauffeur, lawyer and now object of her fantasy, to arrive to collect her. Once more the nerves grew, and she felt sure he would know exactly what she did last night.

Chapter 10

David pulled up on the driveway and before he could get out of the car, Stella had left the house. She locked the door she got into the front passenger seat. She put on her seat belt. It was David who spoke first.

"Morning Stella, you're not hanging around this morning. You OK?"

Stella felt herself flushing knowing why she was nervous and not for the reasons David was thinking, or had he realised and noticed?

"Morning David, no I'm not hanging around. I want to get this nightmare over with and finished. Then I can get back to my real life, the real me. I also don't want to give the neighbours anymore chance to gossip. You know, strange car driven by a man, picking me up. Two and two is thirty-six around here as I am sure you know. I'm OK though. What's going to happen today?"

David was already pulling away to get her away from prying eyes.

"That's OK, as for the neighbours, they'll have more to talk about later. The village post office was burgled last night. Wait 'til they get a sniff of that story, it tops you any day in their eyes, I'm sure." He continued on, "Today we will both go into court, and you will again go into the dock. Apart from your personal details, which you must give, all you need to say is guilty when the clerk reads out the charge. Leave me to do the rest. Now, while we are on our way, you told me a little about the situation last time and more over dinner. Please tell me how the loss of your licence is going to affect your daily life. Oh, and as far as the court is concerned you don't work for me, which is not a lie as I am not paying you."

Stella hadn't thought much about not being able to drive. She pondered life without her car.

"Well," she said. "Without my car work will be difficult as I live in a small village outside town. I will be reliant on the buses and trains. Although the trains aren't bad, it does leave you nowhere near anything that's not directly next to the station. Ipswich is a long walk to town and Bury is not much better. Cambridge is worse, so from a getting about point of view it'll be tricky. The bus service from the village is next to non-existent too. My son is at uni in Edinburgh, so to see him I'll either have to fly from Stansted or take a train for hours and hours. I won't be able to do yoga or go shopping without a great deal of hassle either. It's going to be pretty horrendous. Luckily, I have no mortgage and I do have some income, although it does leave me rather short each month, so I'll have to try and find paid work in order to make ends meet. It won't be easy at my age."

"Excellent. That's all I need to know. Leave it to me and I'll get this sorted out without any problem. Given your reading it comes into the community bracket, but I don't suppose you fancy unpaid work?"

"What? With all the criminals, no thanks."

"Leave that to me also. There's a scheme called the drink drive rehab scheme. It can get you a twenty-five per cent reduction on the ban but costs nearly £200. I'll get the court to offer that to you as well."

They pulled off the dual carriageway at Asda and drove in

the traffic to the centre of town, parking in the spiral car park, two minutes from the court and next to the Wolsey theatre. Stella followed David to the courthouse and let him go through the searches first. As he was well-known, David was only given a cursory search, whereas Stella was properly wanded, and had her handbag checked through as well. Stella walked with David up to the first floor, and David told her to go and sit on one of the benches outside court two. He was sure that was where she would be. Stella did as he asked and there was a real sense of déjà vu as she remembered two weeks earlier and her first visit to the courts. She was sure some of the posse were the same faces as last time, certainly the ushers were, and also the suits who milled about. It was still a deeply depressing place to be. The smell hadn't changed much either, as more people arrived the body odour and stale alcohol became stronger. She saw David talking to another suit, they both glanced Stella's way. *That must be the prosecutor* she thought to herself.

She watched David walk into court two through the airlock and wondered what he was doing. It was a few minutes before he came out.

"OK Stella, let's have a private chat," he said as he walked down the corridor and towards the interview rooms that they had used a fortnight earlier. "You saw me talking with James and he's still onside with this. I've also spoken with the court clerk and we do have Peter judging again today. I want to get you on first and away so we, more you, spend as little time in here as possible. Peter's clerk remembers you and, given how anxious you were last time, has agreed. The other great thing about getting on first is that Peter won't have been pissed off by the regulars, or delayed at the start of the day. That's always a great position to be in. The last thing is, I hope that we're in and out before the press arrive. That way you may even avoid the papers too."

"David, that's great, thank you." He is such a nice man. Every time he does anything, she likes him more and more.

Ten minutes passed and at ten a.m. the usher came and called Stella's name. She went into court as before and into the box. It was the same people that were there the last time and they looked just the same. Stella stood nervously in the dock once more and this time, was able to give her personal details. All the while, David was looking at her and his eyes gave her confidence not to break down. This time. The charge was read out and Stella gulped, looked down at the floor in shame and said "Guilty." She was asked to sit down. She did, she also looked down, head bowed in continued embarrassment as the prosecutor read out the facts of the case to the Judge.

He ended with, "Sir, you may recall this matter from two weeks ago. The defendant was deeply upset, and Mr Hughes asked you to put the case off for the crown to investigate the previous convictions of Mrs Green. The crown have checked the suggestion that her purse was stolen some years ago and indeed this turned out to be the case. Further, Sir, we have had the police check the fingerprints of each conviction that purports to be Mrs Green and although they are all the same fingerprints for each one, they are not the fingerprints for this defendant. This leaves the question, which of them is the real Mrs Stella Green, the lady here or the lady with all the previous convictions. The answer lies with the DVLA, Sir. Their records are clear in that the real Mrs Stella Green lives at the address given by this lady and that she has done so for many years. Her car is registered there, as is her driving licence. Having also spoken with Mr Hughes on this matter both yesterday and this morning, I am satisfied that the lady before you today is the true Mrs Stella Green. She has been caused, as has the crown and this court, a considerable amount of stress and wasted time by the imposter and for that she has the sympathy of the crown." James Purdue sat down and gave way to David, who, when he got a nod from the Judge, stood to give his address.

"Sir, this lady is entitled to the full credit of the court and more. She has now lost her good name, but more than that she has suffered the ignominy of her peers and also the extreme stress of having her actual identity stolen by an unknown person. This is a rare case indeed and I urge you to treat it as such. Mostly those caught for drink-driving suffer the simple consequences that come from the sentencing guidelines, but this lady has suffered more so already. You recall her collapse two weeks ago, and then having to come back in front of you. You in fact yourself said that your displeasure may have been misplaced, and indeed as it transpires it was. This lady came from a good family, a strong business family from Bury St Edmunds, struck by the tragedy of a road accident where both her parents were killed. Her lengthy marriage broke down not three weeks before this incident, caused by solace in alcohol following the discovery of a cheating husband and an argument thereafter. Her good character has gone, as has her family and her social circle, the best of Bury society has turned their backs on her.

As for the future, she is a lady who, although she has a small trust fund income, this does not meet her outgoings, even forgoing things she will no longer be able to do without her driving licence, will need to find employment. She has cut everything to the bone and there is not enough money in her pot. She will have to try and find work. Sir, she hasn't worked for over twenty years, being a mother and housekeeper to her errant husband for all that time. Thurston is a rural village with limited transport links to the rest of the county and wider afield. It is not the worst for public transport, but as Sir knows so well, the desire for the state to provide public transport is not high on their agenda, nor has it been for some years. Essentially this lady will be affected far more than most by the loss of her driving licence, and yes, she should have thought first, but hindsight is both a wonderful thing and also a stick to beat yourself with for a long time to come, and beat herself I have no doubt she will.

As to punishment. She would wish the rehab course, if offered. The guidelines place this at a two-year ban and a community penalty. This is before credit. Does this court really want to put this lady on unpaid work with the rest of the defendants you see day in day out in this courthouse? Surely this case is screaming for financial penalty as the appropriate sentence?" David looked over his shoulder at Stella, winked and sat down.

Peter Snowden spent a few moments before passing sentence. He looked at his iPad, and jotted a few things down, he thought some more, eyes searching above the heads of those in the well of the court for the right thing to do. Then he spoke.

"Stand up, Mrs Green."

She did, weakly and nervously, visibly shaking, she stood and faced the judge. Oh, how she wanted to run. David had said wonderful things, but It was it enough?

"Mrs Green, firstly I need to say it seems I have misjudged you two weeks ago and that will, in part, be corrected today. You have been caused a considerable amount of distress by these proceedings, more than most and I didn't help on that front. It is rare that it comes to light in such a way that someone's identity has been stolen. I do take into account your plea and your loss of good character. I also, to some extent accept the impact on you will be greater than many, but that is also down to you for committing this offence. I accept the pressures impacting on your life that led to the offence. I am also reminded, unusually by this case, of words spoken to me by the former Chief Magistrate when he addressed new deputies some years ago. He said that the greatest gift we have is to be compassionate and merciful. He, of course, was talking about certain cases which are out of the norm and where you, as a judge, could step away from the guidelines to reflect the full situation and do justice leniently where it was appropriate to do so. I find that this is precisely one of those cases. The minimum term I can disqualify you for is one year from driving, I do so. I see no point in you doing unpaid work in the community and so I impose a fine instead, that of £800. With the government tax and costs it totals £965, all to be paid within twenty-eight days please. I will offer the rehab course and I ask Mr Hughes to explain that to you in more detail afterwards. That is all, and you may leave. I doubt that I will ever see you again."

Both Stella and David left the court room and the court building in silence. Once into the fresh air. "Coffee?" said David.

"Yes please." Stella followed David into Ipswich centre and this time they found themselves in Costa Coffee. Two large coffees and a pastry each were ordered by David and they found a seat in the corner.

David confirmed to Stella that she had indeed had a great result earlier. It could have been much worse. The shortest possible ban and a fine, not unpaid work, which would have been the norm for a case such as hers. Why did she not see it that way? Nearly a grand out of pocket and unable to drive for a year did not seem like a great result from where she was seated. At least she could cycle to David's office to work and could get to grips with internet shopping! A tear rolled down her cheek and David used his thumb to gently wipe it away.

"It's not as bad as it seems right now, Stella. Thousands go through this every year. In a week or so you will have got used to it and discovered a new way of making your life work without a car."

Stella told David that she would fulfil her obligation to work off her bill by cycling to work. She was grateful to him for everything he had done so far, it was the shock of the reality now. David reached over the table, touched her hand and tenderly squeezed it. "We'll get you through this, don't worry."

We? We? He said we and he squeezed my hand. Was he being nice? Or did the electricity coursing through her body mean he had feelings for her too? That can't be right, no, she was just a client and he was just being nice. He must do this with all his clients, he's a compassionate man.

David drove Stella home and told her that he would see her tomorrow, she needed to let all this sink in. She thanked him and went inside. Boy, did she need a drink after that morning. Pouring the last glass from the already opened bottle of chenin blanc, she assumed her usual position on the sofa, put the music on, took a mouthful of wine, closed her eyes and let the events of the morning drift away. Stella stayed that way for an hour; chillaxing, letting the music and wine remove her from the reality in which she now found herself. Once the glass was empty and she was totally relaxed, it was time to move. She went into the garage and found, in the corner, her bike. Bought five years ago and ridden as many times. Always sitting there waiting for those good intentions to come into being. Well, now they would have to. How much dust can one bike attract? Still the tyres were inflated. She got a damp cloth and wiped it down, then positioned it, on its kickstand, at the front of the garage, ready to leave the pit lane the next morning.

Later that afternoon, Julie rang. She was calling on her friend to see how the day had gone. Stella gave her a blow-by-blow account of the morning, including the electricity when David squeezed her hand. They talked about how she was going to get about, how she was getting on at work and, of course, David. Julie was delighted that Stella was enjoying her work and that she had such a good boss. She warned her about reading too much into the situation and about getting too involved. It could all end in embarrassment and tears, especially if she was misreading the situation. Take it steady and get to actually know him first. That was good advice and accepted graciously by Stella, but even with the advice she was still hoping inside that she wasn't misreading the situation. They decided that they would meet up in a week or so for a proper catch up. Julie would drive over to Stella and stay the night, if that was all right. She would bring a takeaway and Stella could provide the wine. It was agreed, and was the second non-driving solution that had been found.

In bed, Stella lay on her back. She couldn't sleep even though she was tired. There was a memory playing on a loop over and over, the touch of his hand gently, delicately, removing a tear from her cheek and then the subtle squeeze of her own. Over and over. Turning over, she cuddled the pillow, she could almost feel him, her arms pulling him close, his back against her breasts. She could almost see the back of his head and could almost smell him, there in her bed. Totally comforted by this man in her head, she drifted into a long and restful sleep. She remained in that position all night and when she woke the next morning, he was still there.

Chapter 11

Once Stella had readied herself for work as usual, she remembered that she was cycling to work. This meant it would not be at all sensible to wear her heels and a skirt! She had to change. She put on a pair of jeans and her pumps and changed her top for a T-shirt. Her work clothes were rolled up and placed in her backpack. Stella left the house giving herself an extra twenty minutes for the journey, after all it was only about three miles and she was fit. She rode down the hill and under the railway bridge, this was easy. Along the road to the notorious Fishwick Corner. It was a simple crossroads where accidents were common place; slightly blind to the left, with traffic speeding down the hill from Bury to the right. In a car it's not too bad, but on her bike, even though it's not busy by any stretch of the imagination, it is decidedly tricky and she needed her wits about her. The next mile is a steady incline all the way to Moreton Hall. She didn't realise quite how long this was or quite how many pot holes she would have to dodge. It was hard work for the whole mile. Once at the top, the road became flat and she went from admiring fields and dodging potholes, to looking at the new houses all the way to the office. She only just made it on time, but still had to change. David was already there.

"I thought about giving you a lift but didn't want to intrude on your private life," he said as she walked into the office.

"Thanks, but I think the exercise will do me some good anyway,'" Stella replied. All the while thinking to herself, please pry and intrude into my private life, my personal space and my bed. "Sorry I am a little late, I will get used to this. I just need to get changed." With that she was into the toilet for a quick change while the kettle boiled. Her coffee was already poured and on her desk when she came out. "Thanks for that, David."

Stella spent that day and the next on the invoicing system. She created a file for the bank accounts, a file for the bills, paid and unpaid and a file for the invoices, paid and unpaid. She started on the bank reconciliation and as she did so, matched each entry with the corresponding invoice or bill and moved them into the paid section of their respective files. It was slow and tedious work but by the end of Friday she felt satisfaction and could start to see the wood from the trees. She was understanding his systems and getting to grips with the new terminology she was now having to use. At about half past four on the Friday, David came into Stella's office. It was still a bomb-site but it was now semi-sorted.

"So Stella, how are you getting on? I hope you are managing OK and that I'll see you again on Monday."

She confirmed to David what she had been working on. It was tough, but she was starting to get it under control. By the end of next week, she should be in a much better position, and yes, she was coming back as she still owed him money.

David told her that nothing much would happen between now and five, so she may as well go home. Stella would rather go for a drink with David, but it was too early for her to suggest it and she still knew little about him. He was her boss and she wasn't about to bugger that up just yet. She changed and waved him goodbye with a smile as she left and got onto her bike for the cycle home. The ride home was much easier as it was mostly downhill, except the last four-hundred yards which were a killer uphill that she would get used to and perhaps even start to enjoy at some point. On her way she stopped at the village shop and bought herself a *Bury Free Press*, she was curious.

Having poured the obligatory chenin blanc, Stella settled herself into the chair on the patio and began to read. There wasn't a journalist that she was aware of in the court, but that didn't mean she wasn't famous for the second time in a month. David got several mentions for a variety of cases he had completed. She scoured the paper once and once more. No mention. She had got away with it, she put her face towards the sky and let out a deep breath. The society did not know the result, and nor would they. They would have moved on to other gossip by now anyway. The evening was pleasantly warm as she sat there mulling over the week gone by. It was, by any standard, a very different week. Work, court, a driving ban and a crush! Despite all its difficulties and emotional concerns, on balance, it was in her mind a good week. She had achieved much on a personal level and that delighted her. She could, and would, cope without Tony in her life and she would prove that she didn't need him at all. Even if nothing happened between David and herself, she would still be content and happy. She determined to herself that she would spend the duration of her driving ban getting fitter with more time in the gym and at yoga. Perhaps she might go to that boot camp they do on the village green on a Saturday morning, just not tomorrow though.

Saturday morning came round too quickly. After she did her usual cleaning of the house, she was ready to go to Sainsbury's for the shopping. Then it clicked, "I can't do that, and I forgot during the week. I will have to go online and order the delivery." She sat at her laptop and set up the account, then went through the task of trying to navigate the site to find all her shopping for the next week. It was tricky but she was sure she would get used to it. Sadly though, when it came to the delivery it was not a same day service. She would have to wait until Wednesday for the groceries to arrive after she got home from work. In the interim period she would have to walk to the village Co-op and get some basic provisions to tide her over. Thank god the Co-op had opened the store a few months earlier on the little industrial estate next to the station. Stella readied herself to walk to the shop for the first time in a long time. She took her hessian bags and set off.

The route was simple, out of the road, turn right and follow the road round, nearer than The Fox. As she walked a number of village residents drove past and flashed and waved hellos towards her and she responded in kind. It was a pleasant village where people knew of one another but by and large kept themselves to themselves. They would wonder why she was walking as they had never seen that before and she would give the standard getting fit answer. They would find out eventually, these things always had that nasty habit, but for the time being she would let them carry on in blissful ignorance of the fact she was a criminal. Once inside the store she struggled to find much, other than the basics, but for a few days it would have to do. She saw a few faces she thought she recognised and mutual nods were exchanged but no words spoken. She returned home, somewhat deflated at not having a car and not having the right groceries. This was day three of the ban and the first weekend. Weekends were going to be tough, she thought to herself. Maybe she should have tried that boot camp after all. It would have got rid of a few calories, and some time.

By the time she got home the post had been delivered. There was a card from Brian. It had flowers on the front and said

Thinking Of You. Inside he had written a little note.

"*Hi Mum, saw the card and thought you might like it. I know I don't do cards, but I need you to know that I am here for you whenever and for whatever you need. Just remember that one.*

Love Always, Brian xxx."

Stella welled up and sat in the front room rereading the card several times before closing it and pulling it tight to her chest. She had brought him up so well, she missed him now she was alone and loved him and what he was becoming. There was the usual junk mail from the local food delivery firms who clearly wanted your money and didn't care much for trees. Finally, another letter. She recognised the envelope. Tony's solicitor. This should be interesting.

"Dear Mrs Green,

We note the comments made by you in your last letter. Could we remind you to attempt to keep this matter as civil as possible? We are not in the habit of entering into a point-scoring contest based on accusations and counter accusations. We will put the comments you made down to raw nerves caused by the unfortunate situation you find yourself in and will say no more about it.

We have spoken further with our client. He wishes to get this matter resolved as quickly and amicably as possible. To that end, he will agree for you to petition for divorce based upon his adultery. He will not contest such a petition. To assist we are happy to draft the paperwork for you at our client's expense.

In terms of finances, we understand the total assets of the parties currently stand at around £1,500,000 excluding the trust fund. Our client's salary is currently £80,000 per year with additional bonus, share scheme, dividend benefits and pension.

To reach an early settlement we now propose that you keep

the house, contents and all personal effects. Our client will pay you a further £100,000 over five years by way of clean break.

We hope you will see this as a generous offer and look forward to hearing from you soon.

Yours etc."

She read it twice more and then again with a glass of wine in her hand. Tony was earning more money than she was led to believe, and he had savings that she knew nothing about. This seemed, on the face of it, good money for her. He wanted this done quickly, why? He was normally extremely guarded about money and had said he couldn't afford to pay me a reasonable amount of maintenance. Now he could find £100,000. Something was not right, and she wanted to get to the bottom of it. She worked a bit of it out. £100,000 over five years is the same as her £1000 per month over eight! Did they really think she was that stupid? The house was worth £600,000 tops, so he hadn't really moved on anything at all. She also needed to consider her retirement, what about his pension and what were these bonuses? She had never heard of them.

"Dear Sirs,

Thanks for the letter. I am delighted that he will admit to the world he is an adulterer who has ruined thirty years of marriage by thinking with his penis instead of his brain.

It would appear that he continues to do so when he makes this ridiculous settlement offer. Firstly, the house and contents equates to about a third of the total asset value. Secondly, the lump sum suggestion equates to a little over eight years at £1000 per month. So now your client is trying to REDUCE the settlement to me. I am not a stupid woman, and you may remind your client that when I was working I was PA to a managing director; I ran the office and provided all the financial accounts information. You have your law degrees and I have my business degree, which included financial management. A fool I am not.

I invite your client to revise his offer in the correct direction so as to provide an income for me to retirement and a pension thereafter. In the absence of a sensible costed out offer of at least 50% assets and income at a level I am satisfied with, he will need to provide me with his last P60, last pay slip, current directors contract, current share-holding, current investments and current pension valuation. Once I have that information, I will be able to provide you with my offer of settlement.

Hopefully yours."

She would mull on that for a few days before sending it, let them think I am vaguely interested in allowing him to set up his new life comfortably with his tart. She needed some air after that, so she decided to go down to The Fox. It might be a bit lively with the youngsters in and the herbal qualities of the place would dramatically increase as the night worn on, but they did sometimes have a good band on. Stella straightened her face and put on a more revealing blouse before heading off to the pub. Once there, she found herself with a large glass of wine in the same seat as last time, creature of habit you see. There was a band setting up, she hoped they were a good group. The pub wasn't very full, it was still early, and she was noticed by one of the band. He smiled at her and she smiled back. He was about her age, scruffy with longish hair that looked like it could do with a wash. He was average build and from the way he was setting things up he seemed to be the organiser and drummer for the quartet. She would stay and see how it developed, but if it got too rowdy with the youngsters, she would return home. The drum had the group's name on it – *Play it Again Sam*. She had never heard of them. She ordered another wine from the bar and asked what they were like. Steph, the barmaid, told her they were OK, had played a few gigs there over the last year and normally got a good crowd. They did mainly covers from the '90s onwards.

Once back in her seat by the window she was approached by the drummer who remained standing beside her table.

"Haven't seen you here before," was his rather weak opener.

"I don't come in here that often," Stella replied. "You must be Sam."

"No, I'm Phil, can I get you your next drink. That way we can at least have a crowd of one for the first set."

He must use that line all the time, Stella thought to herself. She needed the outlet of the pub and so why not.

"Yeah sure, thanks. I'm Stella, by the way."

"Great. I'll let them know, see you later."

Phil was as good as his word and on his way back to his drums he stopped at the bar and bought her the next drink. The other band members nudged him and sniggered as he returned to his kit.

They began playing and Steph was right, they weren't too bad at all. Stella was joined by a couple who she didn't know. They introduced themselves as from Ixworth and they were here for the band and a bit of a dance.

For their third number Phil introduced the Madness cover. "It Must Be Love," and dedicated it to, "the lovely Stella by the window," and urged all to sing and dance to it. The lady from the couple looked at Stella and said, "Well he's taken a shine to you, shall we oblige him and have a boogie?"

Stella pondered. "What the hell, let's give him a show." The two ladies got up and started to dance with each other, no handbags, just a little boogie, near the front.

Halfway through the number, the lady said to Stella, "I'm

Lesley, fancy making this a bit hotter for him?" She said looking directly at the drummer. Stella nodded, the wine now taking effect, and the pair turned from regular boogie dancers into erotic lesbians, their hands and arms caressing each other's backs as they held each other closer, lips almost touching. Some hands moved to buttocks and Stella lowered herself to mimic sucking Lesley's breasts, rubbing her head against them while looking at Phil, who could barely play in time, his eyes were firmly fixed on the gyrating couple. At the end of the number, they turned to return to their seats and Lesley gave Stella an obvious squeeze of her buttock before gripping her hand, both wiggling their respective rears provocatively until they reached their seats.

Lesley's other half was unfazed as the two ladies sat and burst out laughing.

"That was some show you put on for him girls. I know I enjoyed it."

"Well, we seem to have hooked the drummer," Lesley replied. "We can go further if you're both game?" She continued with a twinkle in her eye, "How about we pretend to be swingers and invite him to join us after the gig for a foursome?"

"Are you kidding?" spluttered Stella. "I'm not into that. I am strictly heterosexual and have never had group sex, nor do I want to."

"Relax," Lesley said. "Nor are we, but he doesn't know that. We can wind him up during the interval, get it set up so he's distracted completely during the second set and we can leave just before they finish, through the back door. He'll look for us but we'll be gone and his mates will think it's hilarious, as would I. It would serve him right for hitting on you in the first place."

The wine was getting to Stella and in her mild state of inebriation she agreed, as did Lesley's fella. For the rest of the first set they all took it in turns to dance with each other, and all of it was dirty dancing, designed to hook Phil into thoughts of sex. And it did the trick.

At the interval Phil was over like a rocket. He sat down in between Stella and Lesley. He was so horny he could hardly get his words out. This was made all the more difficult by Lesley stroking his thigh. Phil was in male porn heaven at the thought. The group made little small talk but were straight into the plans for later. Phil was so excited that he would have trouble standing given the erection that was now being nursed by Lesley through his jeans under the table where no one could see. Phil readily agreed to meet them after the gig and to follow them back to Lesley's house for drinks and a night of raw passion and debauchery. Phil somehow did manage to return to his drums in order to perform the second set. During it the plotters had various dedications made to them including "Sex On Fire" and "I Want You To Want Me", both poorly performed as, by now, the whole band seemed to be alert to the planned after-party and spent much of their time concentrating more on the outrageous and raunchy dancing performed by the trio of would-be sexual deviants than their playing.

Stella had thoroughly enjoyed the evening and the performance the trio had played towards Phil. They felt the evening was drawing to a close so in turn left the table and the pub by the rear door. In the car park Stella and Lesley swapped numbers and as they hugged to say goodbye, Lesley gave Stella a kiss on the lips, her tongue briefly stroking Stella's lips as she did so. Stella was taken aback, but only slightly due to her alcohol intake and did not respond in kind. Nor did she complain. Stella walked the short distance home, although it was longer than the route there earlier that night. She went straight to bed. Laying there for a few moments, she recalled the kiss from Lesley. Was Lesley hitting on her? Surely not, it was her imagination. They were a good-fun couple though, and she would go to the pub with them again, if Lesley got in touch.

Chapter 12

The next day Stella awoke to a text message from Lesley.
 'Hi Stella, really enjoyed meeting you last night. You are a lot of fun. Would love to see you and do it again, x.'
 Stella was barely awake in bed but by now she was sober. She thought back and remembered the previous night. She remembered the drummer flirting with her, Bill or Phil or something. She remembered dancing and the raunchy dirty-dancing with Lesley. She remembered how alive it made her feel. It was years since she had so much fun and laughed. The thought of the dancing was starting to make her tummy tingle. She remembered the banter and setting Phil up, and she remembered leaving. Leaving the poor sad little drummer boy, who thought he was in for the night of his life, to the shame and no doubt ruthless taunts of his fellow band members when he discovered they had all left him.
 She remembered the kiss. The slight teasing of her lips with her tongue. She had never kissed a girl before, never felt another girl's tongue on her lips. It was curiously arousing for her. But was Lesley hitting on her? Did Lesley want more or was it the drink talking? How should she respond? Should she respond at all? In her state of semi-arousal and curiosity she replied,
 'Hi Lesley, I agree it was a great night and I would love to do it again. If I misbehaved, I apologise, it was the alcohol inside me. Say hi to your man too. Sx.'
 She hit send, then wished she hadn't, but it was too late, the

message had gone. Stella flung herself back onto her pillow. This was crazy, she was heading towards fifty, just came out of a lengthy monogamous marriage, barely slept with another man, let alone had ideas about a woman, and just lost her licence. Now she was working to pay off her lawyer's bill, had a crush on him and was having strange thoughts and flirting with a woman whom she had only just met. What the hell was going on?

No time to think any longer, the phone vibrated, a text message. Stella could barely look. Yes, it was from Lesley.

'So glad you had a good time. If you misbehaved I missed it, mores the pity, perhaps you can misbehave some more later. Sam is going out so I'm free if you want to pop over Lx'

Without thinking Stella replied,

'Sorry Lesley, I can't come over later, I don't drive so I can't get to you. We must do it again soon though x'

Sent. She re-read her reply. She really was encouraging Lesley. What was she thinking? Moments later, ping,

'Well, if you're OK with it, I can come to you, only if you're not busy though x.'

Now she was in trouble. She had started this flirt and it was getting out of hand, although she liked the thought of it, this was new territory for her. If she turned Lesley down, would they go out again and have another laugh? Stella can always put a stop to anything if it gets out of hand. With that Stella sent Lesley her address and between them they arranged that Lesley would come over at two p.m.

Stella spent the rest of the morning in a right quandary. What to wear, what to say, where and when to say it? Whilst all these questions were racing through her mind, she managed to shower but the house was left as it was without the housework being done. Brian rang, and Stella could barely have a conversation with him, her mind was preoccupied. The doorbell rang. Was it two already? Stella opened the door to find Lesley standing there. In the daylight she could see a woman of about the same age, a white blouse, clearly no bra to hide her medium sized breasts, with a fairly short simple skirt and heels. Her face was pretty, blue eyes surrounded by long blonde hair and a petite nose. Stella held open the door and Lesley walked in. Automatically, Stella gave Lesley a hug. Lesley returned the hug tightly with a kiss that went on fractionally too long to be just friendly, or was Stella imagining things again? She led Lesley through to the lounge and offered her a drink.

"Some fresh juice if you have any. Great house."

Stella almost ran to the kitchen and was literally shaking when she poured two glasses of fresh orange. She struggled to carry them back through to her guest, who was sitting on the sofa taking in the room and looking very relaxed. Stella handed her the juice and the pair sat on the sofa facing each other, knees nearly touching.

Lesley took a sip and put her juice down, moving slightly closer to Stella. Their eyes met, and Stella held on tight to her glass. Lesley leant forward to kiss Stella. Stella immediately pulled away.

"Lesley, you need to know that I have never been with a woman. I am open-minded and something stirred inside me last night, but I didn't know if it was the drink and I was misinterpreting the situation."

Softly the reply came, "You weren't, I felt it too, I'll be gentle." Without looking her left hand took the glass from Stella and set it on the coffee table, her hand returned and placed itself gracefully on Stella's cheek before Lesley continued closer and their mouths met for the second time that day. The kiss was soft and lingering. Stella once more felt Lesley's tongue teasing her lips while her stomach started to somersault. Stella allowed her mouth to open and in unison their tongues entwined with each other in a passionate kiss; Stella's first challenge to her sexuality. Stella moaned and placed her hand behind Lesley's head pulling her closer as the kiss lingered on, their mouths refusing to part. Lesley reached down and took Stella's hand, lightly and carefully placing it on her own breast. Through the silk of the blouse Stella could feel Lesley's nipple, erect and wanting. Without thinking, Stella cupped the breast and squeezed her nipple between her thumb and forefinger. Lesley gave a sigh and her own hand sought out Stella's breast which was protected by her bra and T-shirt. Lesley reached down and began to lift the T-shirt up. Stella paused and broke away from the kiss.

"Are you OK?" said Lesley.

"I don't know, but not here, not in this room. The window goes directly to the road outside. Can I take you upstairs?" Stella got up, took Lesley's hand and pulled her to her feet, whisking her upstairs.

They collapsed onto Stella's bed together and once more mouths were engaged, this time more furiously. Lesley returned to the task of removing the T-shirt and unclasping the bra. As it fell away, Stella's breasts were displayed for the first time. Lesley looked in awe and the beautiful full mounds before her and her hand took one in its grasp, Stella moaned in pleasure. She had never felt the touch of a woman and was being driven to the heights of pleasure by this lady. Lesley put Stella on her back and removed her own blouse revealing her breasts to Stella. She lay on top of her and their breasts rubbed against one another while they kissed some more. Lesley's hand sought the button on Stella's jeans, undid it and slid her hand down, inside her knickers and between her legs, feeling the wetness of pleasure Stella was feeling with their encounter.

Stella shuddered as Lesley's fingers entered her. She arched her bottom and allowed Lesley to remove her jeans and panties. She was now naked before Lesley for the first time. Instinctively, Stella reached up and under Lesley's skirt. Lesley was not wearing pants and she tentatively started to explore her new lover with her fingers. Lesley pushed down so Stella was deeper inside her. Lesley moved round and faced away from Stella placing her mouth on top of her sex. She used her tongue on Stella's secret mound, all the while maintaining thrusting movements with her fingers. When she thought Stella was ready to receive her, she straddled Stella allowing her to perform the same act simultaneously. Stella was brought to orgasm and it was a huge, deep, fulfilling orgasm that made Stella cry out. Lesley climbed off and held Stella tight. She was no longer a lesbian virgin.

They lay together for what seemed an age. Laying in silence, allowing Stella to absorb the enormity of what she had – they had – done. Eventually, Lesley turned to Stella and asked, "How are you feeling?"

"Honestly," Stella responded, "truth is I don't know. It's the first time I've done this and I don't know how I feel. A few months ago, I was married and happy, heterosexual, and monogamous. Now I'm separated, have a crush on my male boss and am lying here naked with you having just made love to you. It's all a bit much to take in really. I suppose it's one off the bucket list if nothing else."

Lesley laughed at the final remark. "Yes, I suppose that's one way of looking at it. Just for the record, it's not something I do regularly. Sam doesn't even know. He fantasises like most men about having two women together, but it hasn't happened and I don't want it to. This is my secret, and I've done this with you on the spur of the moment. I hope I can trust you with my secret, I know you can trust me. If this never happens again, I'm OK with that, but rest assured I enjoyed every moment with you, and if you did want to we can meet secretly again. If nothing else, you have a new experience and more than that, hopefully, a new friend."

The duo dressed and went back downstairs where they sat as they had before and continued with their juice as though nothing had happened. They discussed their own lives, likes and loathes and started to learn more about each other. They were remarkably similar in views and outlook. Their encounter wasn't mentioned again. When Lesley left, they gave each other a hug and a kiss, it seemed natural to do so, and said they would stay in touch.

Stella poured herself a much-needed, large glass of wine. She sat at the breakfast bar, no music on, in silence. This had just happened. Why? Would it happen again? When? Was she bisexual? Did she enjoy it? Yes, of course she did. Could she tell anyone? Brian, no never; Julie, I don't know. What of her crush on David, could she go out with him and not tell him? What would he do? What would he say? After all he is a solicitor and they don't do that sort of thing, do they? Was she making it all too complicated and was this a one off? Her life appeared to be spiralling out of control, these things were just happening, and she could do nothing to stop them. This was such a far cry from her life only months before. She had been in a steady, normal, loving life (so she thought) relationship without any complications until Tony left. Was this all happening because Tony was gone, she was released, or just vulnerable. Confused as she was, Stella decided she was having fun and apart from the loss of her driving licence, things were going OK and she was happier than she had previously been. She now had a job with a great boss, and men and women were hitting on her left right and centre. It was as though she had a neon sign with an arrow pointing at her saying, 'now available, come and fuck me nicely.'

Chapter 13

The next morning Stella rode her bike to work as normal and she felt strangely uplifted by the events of the weekend. She had a new energy about her. What she didn't know was, why? Was it the evening in The Fox and winding up the drummer on Saturday? Was it the encounter with Lesley on Sunday that left her confused and fulfilled? Or was it the fact she was going to work and going to see David that had her so perky? She didn't know and, frankly, didn't care. All she knew was, she felt good, the best she had felt in weeks, and that was all that mattered at that moment.

She arrived at the office and parked her bike, unlocked and went in. It wasn't long before David arrived. He asked about her weekend and Stella told her she had enjoyed a live band on the Saturday night and saw a friend on Sunday. She was sure she blushed, if she did, David said nothing. David explained that it had been a long weekend and he had spent much of it in the police station on a serious rape case. A lad called Bob Stocker, who studied geography at Cambridge, had been arrested for a rape following a university party. His alleged victim was a fellow student. He had been bailed by the police until Friday, but David expected him to be charged and remanded to court on Saturday. He also dealt with Ian James, a regular scrapper, who got drunk in LP nightclub and decided in this drunken bravery that he could win in a fight with a member of door staff. He was always going to lose as he is only five feet eleven inches and build like spaghetti, but he does love to fight when he's had a drink. He had been remanded and would be in court this morning. David explained he had popped in to do his legal aid online application before heading off to court. Stella asked if she could watch and learn, and David thought that was a good idea. They sat in David's office and Stella watched patiently as David filled in the numerous pages online and then pressed the submit button. Stella tried to concentrate, but thoughts of being close to him and events of Sunday afternoon kept momentarily distracting her from the task.

David set off for court and Stella returned to her own office after making a coffee. She continued with her task of getting the accounts and other books straight. She had completed the bank reconciliations and tied them all up with the outstanding invoices and payments in. Even the legal aid schedule seemed to be going well for her. The office phone rang, and Stella thought to herself, '*it's got to be done sometime,*' so she answered. It was Bob Stocker. He was in a terrible state and extremely concerned, wanting to speak to David urgently about his case. Stella confirmed that she knew about his case and that David was in court for the morning at least. She took his phone number and told Bob she would get David to call as soon as he returned from court.

'*Phew,*' she thought, '*I've taken a call, spoken to a rapist and not threatened to cut his balls off. That wasn't so bad.*' She went back to her files and discovered that there were several police station, magistrate's and crown court files that appeared to be finished but not billed. In fact, there were quite a number of them, mostly magistrate's court files, some going back several months. She made a list of them and the date she thought they were finished. She would go through them with David later. Stella took two more calls that morning, one a sales call and the other from a woman, clearly drunk, who called herself Lacey or something. Stella told her to call back later, (she meant when sober but didn't want to antagonise the woman who may have simply had a speech impediment.) She also spent her time sorting the files and the filing cabinets. By the time she had finished, her office looked, for the first time since she had started, like an office. Stella felt proud of her achievement. She took five, and checked her phone. Two texts. One from Julie wanting to confirm for Friday night, and one from Lesley asking how she was after Sunday. She went back to Lesley first.

'*Hi, Lesley. Thanks for the concern. It was my first time, so I was left with a rollercoaster of questions and emotions as you can imagine. Now I've had time for it to sink in, I can say I really enjoyed it and if you want to, we can meet again. Sx*'

Send.

The reply was quick.

'*Wow, I wasn't expecting that. Yes please. Making love to you and taking your lesbian virginity was an honour. I also really enjoyed it as well. How long do you want to leave it? Days, weeks? Up to you Lx*'

'*Oh, please days, before the nerves set in and I back out. I can do you dinner. How does that sound? Sx*'

Was the equally quick response.

Lesley confirmed that Sam was going on a night out with the boys, some stag do or other on Thursday, and that would fit with her just right. She could come over about seven. It was agreed, Stella was to have her second encounter this Thursday.

Stella went back to Julie and made plans for her to come round on Friday night. Julie would stay over, and they would have a catch up and a gossip.

My god, her social life had not been like this for an age.

Now Stella seemed to be at a loose end. She decided to tidy the office up. She hoovered and polished away at the reception area. She had a new-found energy. All the while the thought of Lesley was never far from her mind. Now she had two crushes, one a man and the other a woman.

David returned to the office just before lunch. He was amazed at how tidy it was in the reception area and Stella's office. Stella made him a coffee and they sat in his office eating their lunches together. Stella explained all the progress she had made and how she had organised the files. David was impressed with what she had done and seemed pleased with her efforts. Once they had finished their lunch, between them, they went through Stella's list of unbilled files. David informed her that police station and magistrate's files finished within the last month would go on the next billing run. Those files were put in the 'Awaiting Billing' drawer. The crown court files were sent away for costing and so those that were finished could be posted out to the costs draughtsman. Stella took the details of where to send them and said she would get that sorted. There was a pile of about twenty files left which were still to be decided upon. David confirmed that in each case they had slipped through the net. Those over three months old were simply too late, but those less than three months old could be billed. David estimated those files that could still be billed alone added up to about £4000. He thanked Stella as they would have all been missed and by finding them, she had more than paid off the 'bill' she was working for. They would talk later in the week about a new arrangement.

Stella remembered the phone calls. She told David about Bob Stocker and he confirmed he was worried for his future. Nothing he could do except wait for the police to make up their minds, but he would call him. Lacey, was probably Tracey Murphy. She was an alcoholic prostitute whom he had acted for for years. It was about time she gave up alcohol, and age were taking their toll and she couldn't be getting that much business these days. Stella thought that was mildly amusing. She still hadn't got to grips though with the fact that David was so blasé about these people who were the dregs of society and largely ignored or worse, unknown, to most of the local inhabitants of Bury St Edmunds. This was a real eye opener for her.

She asked David how the police station and magistrate's files were billed and David said he spent one Saturday a month in the office, ploughing through them. She suggested he train her to do them and legal aid applications to fill her time. David thought that was an excellent idea. He was due to do the billing the week after next so that would be a good time to learn, if she didn't mind working a Saturday. He would of course buy her lunch and pay her for her time. Something else in the diary then. What a busy day this was turning out to be!

Later that afternoon, he sat Stella down and did some 'dummy' legal aid applications. He explained to her the pitfalls to watch for, and the shortcuts. Stella took notes and even some precedent wording she would need for the interests of justice page, where you have to justify legally why the client needed a lawyer. It was tricky, but with a little practice she knew she would be able to deal with all of this for him. David sent her home early as she had done so much. Stella took him up on the offer and set off down the road and back to hers.

When she got home, she was exhausted. She decided on a long soak in the bath and an early night. She needed it. All this planning a social life was sapping her energy. That and working for a living. She wondered how people managed to fit it all in.

The bubbles, warmth of the water and the obligatory glass of wine soothed her to deep relaxation. She found herself wondering about her future. What was to become of her? Would she find someone else to share her life permanently, would she ever trust someone sufficiently to allow that to happen? It was a wonderfully relaxing bath and all the cares seemed to drain from her body. While considering her future she decided that she must get herself back into yoga, before too much time passed and then she would find it difficult to regain her motivation. That was her next goal, if she could fit it in!

Tuesday and Wednesday were uneventful. Work was up to date, so there was little to do. She sent Brian an email updating him on the last few weeks, his father's lawyers, the forthcoming meeting with Julie and work. She even mentioned the story about The Fox, he would chuckle at that one, she was sure. By Thursday, Stella was a bundle of nerves once more. She was anticipating her meeting with Lesley and was again questioning her sanity in arranging the meeting. Her work was muddled, but thankfully she was on top of things so had the time to take a steadier pace and double, and even triple, checking what she was doing.

The ride home was also tricky. All she could think about was Lesley. She was not concentrating on what she was doing and was very nearly knocked off her bike several times as she veered too far out from the curb. By the time she realised she had missed Fishwick corner and not turned left at it, it was too late. She pressed on and decided to continue at the next junction towards The Fly (the only other pub in Thurston, actually called The Victoria but known as The Fly for reasons lost to the mists of time) and down the hill to home.

By the time the knock on the door came, Stella had managed

a shower although her hair was still wet and she was still in her robe. She had also remembered the draft letter to Tony's solicitors. She reread it and was happy, so she printed it off and popped it in an envelope ready to send the next time she left the house. Lesley was given a hug and kiss when she arrived and Stella offered to go and get dressed. Lesley said she didn't have to, so she didn't. Dinner was in the oven and while they waited, Stella took the opportunity to sit with Lesley on the patio, allowing the sun behind her to dry her hair. She could see Lesley looking at Stella with her legs poking out from the bottom of the robe and saw her eyes follow her body slowly up, taking in each part of her. The robe was only loosely fastened and it gave Lesley a glimpse of her breasts beneath. Stella's face was relaxed, and she tilted her head back to allow the sunlight to get to as much hair as possible.

They chatted generally until dinner was ready and then went inside to eat. Lesley was on her second glass of wine and Stella reminded her about drinking and driving. They sat down and enjoyed southern fried chicken with a freshly made salad. Stella's robe loosened further as she ate and, although she didn't know it, her breast was now exposed to Lesley. Lesley told Stella that Sam was not expected home that night so, if Stella was comfortable, she could stay all night. Stella said that was fine, and wine no longer became an issue.

After dinner Stella asked Lesley if she fancied a bath to which she said yes, and the duo went upstairs. While Stella ran the bath Lesley made herself comfortable on the bed once again, and Stella joined her while they waited. They used the opportunity to kiss and embrace each other. The bath was done and the bubbles were in. Stella disrobed and jumped straight in, taking her wine with her. She was followed quickly by Lesley who handed Stella her glass of wine. The bath was double size so there was plenty of room for both to recline and relax. The music was playing softly in the background, each admired the other and there was leg stroking by each of them, turning the atmosphere electrically sexual. Stella was now very turned on and she wanted to smell touch and taste all of her once more. Sensing the urgency, Lesley suggested they get out of the bath and relax in bed.

They dried each other and found themselves under the duvet and holding hands. Stella made the first move by rolling towards Lesley and putting her tongue inside Lesley's mouth. The two lovers spent the next hour in slow sensual love making: touching, caressing and kissing, sometimes simply holding each other and feeling each other's naked bodies. This night was not a night of raw passion like Sunday afternoon, but an emotional ride for both of them to enjoy at a beautifully relaxed pace and in a discovering manner. At some point in the embrace, Stella released her hold on Lesley and turned her back on her. She leant over to the bedside table and took something out. When she turned back to face Lesley, she was holding a vibrator.

"Would you mind?" she asked.

Lesley simply took the vibrator from Stella and began to use it gently, rubbing outside and around Stella's wanting and wet vagina. After teasing her for a few minutes, Stella's hand joined Lesley's and between the two of them the vibrator was placed inside Stella. Stella took Lesley's hand away and continued on her own, bucking and moaning in pleasure. Before she came, she withdrew and returned the favour to Lesley. This time she made sure that Lesley was fully satisfied before she stopped. The vibrator was placed back in the drawer, and the lesbian lovers continued, unabated and with more vigour until they both collapsed with exhaustion. There they remained in an embrace of total fulfilment.

The next thing Stella knew was the sound of her alarm. She woke up and turned to find Lesley still beside her. She cuddled her close and stroked her face and hair, a sign of appreciation and contentment for the night before. Lesley stirred, and Stella got up and made them both a coffee. Lesley thanked her, and Stella replied, "No, thank you. Last night was the most enjoyable night I have had, on so many levels, for a long time." She meant every word. They washed, dressed and Lesley left. Stella got her things ready for work and left also.

After work, Stella returned for a night with Julie. That would be interesting, since their last meeting Stella had slept, quite literally, with a woman, and she didn't yet know how Julie would react, if indeed she even told her about it.

When Julie arrived, she was carrying a take away. "Chinese," she announced. "My treat."

"Great," said Stella. "Saves me cooking. Just the wine to pour and the plates to warm then."

They ate their food and drank their wine, all the time the chatter never stopped. It had always been that way with the two of them. Julie thought *the evening in The Fox was absolutely hilarious* and thought *she may have seen that band before*. She told Stella, "Next time, make sure I am invited."

They talked about work and how much money Stella had recovered for David. No, there was no hint of romance there, yet. Yes, she fancied him and no, he had not made a move, but he was going to offer her a full-time job. And so, it continued into the late evening. Both ladies were getting tipsy and without thinking Stella said to Julie, "Have you ever been unfaithful?"

Julie said "No, no other man has been near me since two years before my wedding. Why?"

"What about a woman?"

Julie sobered up a bit at this line of questioning. "No, never. Why do you ask?"

Stella thought carefully before saying, "I'm just curious. Now I'm on my own the world's my oyster as they say. I wondered if you ever had thoughts of being with another woman, you know, sexually. They say it's a common fantasy."

Julie responded, "Stella, I hope you are not suggesting…? Well, I'll be honest with you since we have always been so, and shared our deepest thoughts and confidences before, yes, I have thought about it. There is something naughty and erotic about the whole thought. You see it often enough now in films and it's no longer taboo. In fact, many are quite open about it. So yes, it has crossed my mind. I personally don't think I have the bottle to try though. What if I didn't like it, or did it wrong? I think it would have to be with a complete stranger to avoid the embarrassment of the next day. Maybe if I was very drunk in a club in London, you know, that sort of thing."

Stella agreed with Julie and held back the truth. "I'm glad you said that because it means I'm not weird. Over the last few weeks, I've been curious myself. Maybe the lack of sex has got my mind going to places it ought not to go. Like you, it's a matter of bottle though, and at our age too!"

They both decided it was a pleasant fantasy and unlikely to happen to either of them, but being curious is normal and good for the mind and the body to think of other things. Maybe the next time either of them had sex they might use it as an opportunity to have a little fantasy in their heads and pretend it wasn't a man they were with, they laughed.

The conversation returned to more mundane matters and eventually, the two went their own way to their own beds. Stella went straight to sleep.

Chapter 14

The next morning Stella woke late, and by the time she had reached the kitchen, Julie was already there. She had raided the fridge and breakfast was set out for Stella. Fresh orange, a pot of coffee, yoghurt, honey, fruit, and she could smell the bacon, which must be in the warming drawer. Their relationship was such that this was no problem for Stella or Julie and both knew this would not cause offence. Julie knew Stella would be grateful, and she was.

They sat and enjoyed yoghurt while the eggs were busy scrambling themselves and the toast was, well, toasting! The fresh coffee would be nicely done in the press.

From nowhere Julie turned to Stella and smiling at her said, "Bitch."

"What the hell have I done now. Christ, I've only just got out of bed!"

"You, talking about lesbians last night. I couldn't sleep and kept mulling it over in my mind. Shit Stella, I was turning myself on at the thought of going to London for a weekend and finding a beautiful girl to turn the fantasy into a reality. What have you done to me?"

Stella laughed back, "Well, if you can get away for the weekend we can go to town and see if we can find a club for you to live out your fantasy. I'm game if you are. If nothing else we'll have a bit of fun for a night, away from everyone here, which will be good for me, that much I do know." She would enjoy a weekend away but was not thinking about Julie as yet another lover.

Julie confirmed she would work on it and if she could swing a night in London they would go and have a great night away from it all. They finished breakfast and Julie left to go home to her husband and daughter, vowing to get back to her in the next few days. Stella did her Hinch on the house and was satisfied with the results. She was in need of a rest, so she planned to sit out the rest of the day. Catching up with emails, watch a film, anything to veg and get some energy back. The shopping she would do online, so she didn't have to go out at all.

She had a reply from Brian. He was delighted his mum was doing OK. Stella was right, he thought the drummer's tale was hilarious. Studies were back up to date, and he had a girlfriend. Ellie was her name, a second-year economics student. He was rather struck on her and had been seeing her for a few weeks now. They were getting close. *"Close,"* Stella thought. *"After a few weeks what did he know, really young love was just that. A few more years of maturity and he may realise what love actually was. Still, it was nice that he had a girlfriend, someone he could share things with."* She composed a reply informing her son that she hoped to meet this Ellie soon. She told him about her job and how nicely it was progressing, that she needs to get into yoga again and find classes that suited her work. The bike was great for her general health, and Julie had stayed again last night. That was him caught up.

Mid-afternoon the phone pinged with a text message. David. He was apologetic for not talking to her as promised in the week and if she was free, they could meet for a meal in a pub. Nothing special, but he did want to talk to her. Stella needed an early night to recover from the last few days. She told David that would be fine, but she didn't need a late one! He agreed to pick her up at half six and they would go to the Norton Dog, a pub in the next village and about five minutes from Stella's, a pub with a decent reputation for reasonably priced food. That was that. *"Great,"* thought Stella. *"As if my life isn't complicated enough."* But she was enjoying all this attention. She had a shower and pulled on some jeans and a tight T-shirt. The Dog was OK, but not the sort of place where you dress up. It was certainly not a romantic venue.

David duly turned up on time, as he always seemed to do, dressed casually in jeans and sweatshirt, smelling divine. He apologised again and drove Stella to the pub.

"My god, this guy is hot. Even hotter than Lesley," she thought, as she watched his thighs while he changed gear in the car.

They found a table in the main part of the pub, where the tables offered a little more space between them and the two of them both decided a burger was the order of the day.

David started with a speech. "Stella, this is difficult. When I saw you as duty solicitor, I felt something in you. I felt a spark, but I also saw your vulnerability and your intelligence. Stella, you are a very pretty lady and I would love to see more of you socially. I am taking a big risk telling you this. Firstly, you were a client and one can't date clients. Secondly, you are working for me and that's another big no-no. I am faced with a bigger dilemma because the things you have done in the office are fabulous and you could do so much more. I truly don't want to lose you as a member of staff. The thing is do I ask you out? Or do I offer you a full-time role with me? I've wrestled with this over the last few days in my mind. I hope that you will stay with me at work and I want to offer you a job. I hope you can accept, and also accept that in doing so you will be working for a man who would like more, a possible relationship that simply can't be. I will pay you £24000 per annum and give you five weeks holiday, plus bank holidays. But if working with me in the knowledge that I also like you as a person, no, as a beautiful woman, then we can part company, but I fear that would be to both our detriments."

Stella was dumbstruck, her mouth felt as though it had hit the floor. What to say? The best she could come up with was, "David, my god, that was not expected. I had no idea you felt that way and I am truly flattered. I know nothing about you, other than you're a solicitor. I have loved the last two weeks working off my debts, it's given me a new focus and started to restore my confidence in my own abilities. Yes, I would love to continue to work for you. Thank you so much." She wasn't about to reveal her desires for him. She continued, "We've spoken and you have played the game with the society, you know all about me but of you I know so little. You are a lovely kind and generous man."

David thought, *yes Stella was right, they had met several times and worked together for two weeks now and he hadn't told her anything about himself.*

"OK, you're right, now is as good at time as any." With that, David began. He told Stella he was an only child, aged fifty-seven. He had been a solicitor since university, and decided to specialise in criminal defence work, as he wanted to help. He knew it wasn't the fat-cat lawyer way, but he wanted to try and work for the underdog and to be frank, he loved the thrill of the court room and criminal defence work was the best, well virtually the only, way to get lots of court time. He had been around Bury all his working life. He was married a long time ago, but that marriage failed. It was his working that caused the marriage to break up. He was at work all week and in the evenings was spending so much time in the police station with almost the same at weekends that the strain was too much for the marriage to stand. He was regretful, but it was his career and couldn't think to change it. That was over twenty years ago now. His ex-wife had moved away to London and, he thought, had remarried. They were not in touch. They had no children, which he regrets now. He had other relationships, but they didn't last for the same reason. Working for himself and latterly with no support, rather ruins any chance of a meaningful relationship. Now, at fifty-seven, he was looking to relax more and certainly stop evenings and weekends. He had people he can call upon to cover those, but with little social life to speak of he still tended to do much of the work himself. It's a catch-22 at the moment to relieve boredom and it's what he'd always done. He lived in a lovely house on Northgate Avenue, four bedrooms and nice garden to relax in. No pets. Loves cooking. At the end he said simply, "Have I missed anything?"

Stella smiled and said, "No, I don't think you have."

"So, from Monday, you are officially an employee. Hmm, practice manager I think would be a good title to describe you. I am really looking forward to a great working future together. The only downside will be the staff Christmas party. It may be slightly limited by the numbers attending." David said with a chuckle.

They finished their meal and David returned Stella to her home. Stella invited David in for a celebratory drink and he politely declined and went on his way.

"*Well*," thought Stella. "*I have the hots for David and now I know he has the hots for me.*" This new life is still developing quite nicely. It was a shame that he was stuck with the new vogue that he couldn't have a relationship with her, but she could work on that in time. After all, they would be consenting adults and surely that was all that mattered, wasn't it? Stella relaxed with a glass of wine to herself. It had been an interesting day when all was said and done. A girlie weekend in London in the offing, and now a job that secured her finances, Tony didn't know about it and with a gorgeous boss who wanted into her pants. Yes, a very good day all round. An early night was called for to recover from the last few days. Stella went to bed and slept extremely well once more, she was exhausted.

She woke late on Sunday morning and she once more felt the new lease of life that was breathing into her on a daily basis. Stella spent the day on her laptop sorting out the shopping, answering emails, paying bills. One email was from the travel company. It informed her that all the plans were now in place and here was the full and final itinerary for her safari. To confirm the final details, she had to go online and input her advance passenger information. It also advised that she would need a number of injections to protect herself while abroad; typhoid, yellow fever, hepatitis a and b, tetanus and she should get some anti-malaria tablets to take from a few weeks before she travelled until after her return. She had almost forgotten about her revenge safari in all the excitement of the last few weeks. She duly completed her API as requested and used the online facility with her GP to make an appointment for her jabs. It was only two months away now. Her clothes and camera should be delivered soon as well. She would have to remember to book the time off with David, holiday pay – this was crazy!

In addition to this, she remembered she had to book her drink-drive rehabilitation course. Stella went to their website and realised that it was a series of appointments that she would have to go to. She booked the start for two weeks after she returned from safari, to give herself time to get over the potential jet-lag. Following that, she remembered she wanted to get back into her yoga. She looked at the various options in the area, starting with the self centre. It needed to fit in with her work and also be near enough to cycle to. She found a great Hatha class that started at six p.m. and thought she could hang around after work and do it before going home. She knew the cycle ride home would be a bit of a killer after yoga, but hey, needs must. She also looked at Unit 1 and considered joining their boot camp programme, but decided to leave that until another day. Given her mobility issues for the next few months, her time was precious enough, especially with her new and fast-developing lifestyle.

Having accomplished a great deal that day, Stella poured herself a glass of wine and sat content in her lounge. She couldn't help but to think about Lesley and her new sexual discovery. She hadn't heard from Lesley since she left, and she hoped that it was not the end of the relationship. Stella picked up her phone and opened her messages. She found the message trail from Lesley and there had been nothing. She was missing her. It had only been a few days, but she found herself wanting interaction with her. David was another matter, but at the moment she didn't have to choose between them as David had not yet happened, sadly. Stella sent Lesley a text. Nothing requesting another night or afternoon of passion, just a message to say hi and to keep in touch. She hoped it wouldn't be too long before she got a reply. With the thought of David on her mind, she decided to send him a text too. She simply apologised for texting and hoped he didn't mind but she wanted to thank him for the meal and the job offer. Again, she hoped he would also reply.

It was David who got the first reply in. He confirmed that she should feel free to text whenever she wished to, and no need to apologise. He looked forward to seeing her in the morning. She responded simply thanking him, and left it there for now. Stella's glass was empty, so she filled it up and sat back to chill as the afternoon headed towards the evening. She contemplated a walk to The Fox, but decided to give it a miss, she didn't want to be seen to become a regular. Instead, she put on a chill-out compilation, reclined herself on the sofa and let the world and its dog simply pass her by. She did miss being able to drive, but thought she was doing OK and not going too stir crazy at her restriction. The wine and the soft music helped her to unwind and she soon felt her eyelids struggling to remain open. It was only seven thirty but she decided the best thing for her was to have a quick bath and get an early night. This new life was exhausting her. Was it the sex, the cycling, the mental challenges of the new job? She didn't know but believed it would sort itself out in due course.

Having bathed and clambered into bed, she went to put her phone onto charge and noticed a message. She hadn't heard it go off. Must have been while the bath was running. It was Lesley.

"Sorry I haven't been in touch. Sam was arrested on his night out. The lads got drunk and it got messy. His solicitor sorted it out and he got a caution on Saturday morning. Bloody idiot. I've been dealing with him ever since and making him pay. Very embarrassing. Seems we have got over it now though. Do you fancy The Fox next Friday night? They have a different group on, bit heavy but good with it."

Stella replied, she was sorry about Sam but glad it was sorted. Yes, she would love Friday night and if they both wanted to drink they could stay at hers, if Lesley didn't mind. Lesley responded with a thanks for the invite, she would talk to Sam and see. She reminded Stella that Sam didn't know and it needed to be kept that way. Stella confirmed that the secret was safe.

With that, Stella rolled over and hugged her pillow, pulled the duvet tight and went to sleep with thoughts of David, and work, and fonder thoughts of Lesley.

Chapter 15

Stella woke with the alarm as normal and while laying there, realised it was a new day and slowly coming out of her sleep, she remembered this was her first day at her new, employed, job with David. Excitement grabbed her, even though she had been doing the work for a few weeks it somehow felt strange, different. It was a new beginning. A time when she knew she could stand on her own two feet and could manage financially. It was a good feeling.

She cycled to work with a renewed enthusiasm, and the journey seemed somehow easier than it had previously. David was already at the office when she arrived.

"Coffee for the manager?"

"Oh my god, the manager," she laughed out loud, she was the manager of herself. "Yes please, boss!"

Stella went into her office and in the middle of her desk was a huge bunch of flowers.

"A welcome to the business gift. Here is your coffee, but I won't make a habit of it." David giggled.

The pair were getting on well and developing a good business relationship. David said he was off to court and he had left some police station cases from the last week or so in her tray. Could she put them onto the system and get them ready for billing? That was no problem for Stella. As David left for court he stopped in the open doorway and looked back over his shoulder to see Stella watching him go. Both of them smiled.

Stella settled into her desk and pressed on with her work. First, she checked the bank account and reconciled the last week's transactions. She was pleased with herself that she was up to date, and doing it weekly made it much easier, and also meant a better financial picture was possible. She looked at the outstanding bills that were due to be paid and decided that there was more than enough money in the account to discharge them. The account was looking healthy, but it was an illusion. David only ran two accounts, an office account and a client account. The client account was off limits and always fairly low in any event. The office account was the healthy one, but this account also held the VAT money which built up over a quarter and then was devastated when the VAT was then paid.

She had to ensure there was at least the VAT money in the account. Stella ran the VAT report and it showed that once the VAT currently owed was paid, they would be in the red. This was not a situation she would ever tolerate in her own account and would do her level best to make sure it didn't happen at work. To her, this was a sign of failure. She looked again at the bills due to be paid. There were a few that could wait, agents that had done the work, but David hadn't even sent the bills in to the LAA yet. This was another thing she would need to talk to David about.

She put that work to one side and began to put the new clients onto the system. There were several over the course of the last week or so, mostly work done by David and a handful by agents on his behalf. Some didn't have outcomes, so she couldn't tell if they could be billed. She needed to know so using her initiative, she decided to ring the police investigation centre directly. She spoke with Steve, a detention officer. He was most unhelpful, a real jobsworth who was far too busy to deal with her. Stella thought to herself, *another arrogant copper, she knew how* to deal with arrogant men. Down the phone she started to cry, she told Steve this was her new job, she needed it to get herself off benefits and bring up her kid without the absent father who beat her badly. She must keep the job and her boss had said he needed the information before he got back from court, please Steve, please, it won't take long. By the time she had finished with Steve, she had a new friend, one who would do anything to help her, just call, anytime, and if you need a private chat, hey, let me know. What a slime! But a slime that Stella now had in her pocket. David would be pleased that every police station matter could now be billed, and he was going to show her how to do it. David didn't return to the office that day. Instead, he phoned to apologise that he was stuck at court, but he would see her in the morning.

When Stella got home, she poured a glass and checked the post. Another letter from the solicitor's. This was a quick response. She opened it, took a slug of wine and read it:

'*Dear Mrs Green,*

We must once more ask you to refrain from hurling personal insults directed at our client. It is a difficult enough situation for you both and insults will not help it any.

As regards the divorce, we are agreed that you can file for our client's adultery. He will not defend it and will reimburse you the court costs. We repeat our offer to assist on the preparation of the paperwork.

Regarding the finances, our client is genuinely trying to be helpful and reach an amicable settlement. He repeats his offer and amends it in the following terms:

1. The house is transferred to you outright;
2. The contents are retained by you;
3. He will pay you a lump sum of £100,000 within 28 days

of the order being made;
  4. He will pay you a further £100,000 in 18 months' time
  5. He will pay £250,000 from his pension into a pension fund of your choosing.

The reason for the delayed payment at four is because he will need to encash some shares bought under the company share scheme agreement. Encashment before 18 months brings with it rather large tax bill which he would wish to avoid.

We think you will find this a much improved offer and we have advised our client that this is more than generous given his finances.

This is on a clean break arrangement.
We look forward to hearing from you,
Etc.'

Stella had to read it twice and twice more before it sank in. This was a substantial increase of heading towards 50% on the previous offer. Although she knew she would have to take it seriously, she was wondering what he was up to. There was no way he was going to roll over and give her a penny more than she was entitled to. No matter what offer was made, it would be to Tony's advantage in some way, she knew that, but what else was there? He would hide as much as possible if she was too greedy and she may end up with less. The question was, how far could she push it before he turned nasty about it? She would need to take a bit more time over this one.

Julie text. She had good news. How did Stella fancy a night, or two, in London end of next week? Yes it was to get her bucket list ticked off!

OMG, Julie was serious, and it was her fault. Well, it was working for Stella, so why should she deprive Julie of the opportunity? Why the hell not? It could be a major celebration, the letter she had received confirmed, no matter what, her future was assured, at least financially. Yes, she would go, they would go and see what happened. If nothing else, it would be a good laugh away from the society, who she hadn't heard from or seen for some time now, and that was refreshingly good.

She decided to take the bull by the horns, Stella used the evening to do a little research. If this trip to London was going to be as much fun as possible the right pubs and clubs needed to be found. If Julie was going to find a woman to experiment with, they would need to be in the right place, and frankly, Stella had no idea where to go. She was, after all, very new to this only ever having had Lesley to show her the way. Stella reached for the laptop and searched 'lesbian pubs and clubs in London', if anyone ever saw her browser history, she would have questions to answer that was for sure. The mass of results that came from the search was incredible. She was surprised by the sheer number of bars and clubs to choose from. Thinking about it for a moment her surprise waned. She shouldn't have been surprised, it was just that she had never given it a thought at all, and why should she have? Having looked at a few websites she decided a good starting point would be the Admiral Duncan in Soho. If that was proving problematic, then She Soho which was fairly close by. If they couldn't pull in either of those, they were in trouble. Now for lodgings. Where to stay. Somewhere decent but not too overpriced and relatively nearby. As luck would have it, she found an apartment in Soho with two double bedrooms for £350 a night. That was great, both she and Julie would enjoy that far more than a hotel room each. "*Well,*" she thought to herself. "*This is going much better and far easier than I thought.*" Having made the decision, Stella booked the flat and text Julie to confirm the arrangements. They would drive to Epping and pick up the tube from there. All sorted. Julie came back quickly and full of excitement. It was in the diary, that means it was happening.

The next morning Stella cycled to work, it was colder. She had taken a backpack with her Lycra inside and planned to go to the self-centre for a yoga class at six. She must get back into the swing of a fitness regime. She hoped David wouldn't mind her staying in the office until her class. Once more David had beaten her to work and greeted her with a cheery smile as he went, again, to make her a coffee.

"This is becoming a habit," he laughed.

Stella was slightly embarrassed and apologised.

"I was joking," he replied. "Don't worry about it. Let's make a rule. First one in makes the coffee."

That was agreed. David had no court hearings that day so was due to be in the office. They had a meeting.

They discussed the police station cases and David was impressed with her use of initiative to get the information from the police. He decided to use the day to start to teach Stella how to get the matters costed onto the spreadsheet to be uploaded to the LAA for payment at the end of the month. David showed her a few, reminding her that these were easy as the fee was the same for each one, unless it was only a telephone advice, in which case it was a fixed £30. The important thing was to make sure she claimed the mileage, as this was extra and important as it would need to be paid out to the agent. These mileages added up and could end up being a substantial loss. Given her history in financial accounting this was not rocket science to Stella, but she said nothing, just nodding in the appropriate places. David watched Stella do some herself and he was impressed at how quickly she picked it up. He was about to leave her to it, when Stella stopped him. "I know I have just started work for you but

I need to tell you, and it slipped my mind in the pub the other day, I have a holiday booked already. It's in two months' time and it's for three weeks. I hope that's OK?"

David thought for a moment, "In two months you will be running this place and there'll be no need for me probably. I would think that everything will be far more up to date and three weeks away will do you good after everything. Go and enjoy the break. Just make sure you come back to me."

"Deal, and thank you." Without thinking she leant towards him and kissed him on the cheek. Immediately realising what she had done she said, "Oh my god, I am so sorry, it was a natural reaction of thanks for being such a kind man, err, boss, I mean, you know."

"Stella, stop digging. It's fine and also most pleasant. Thank you too." She watched David make a hasty retreat to his own office before something that shouldn't happen, did.

It was lunchtime before they saw each other again, both stayed in their respective offices, Stella not wanting to face David until she had cooled down. She remained a little excited and embarrassed, but didn't know if David was feeling the same. David came into Stella's room with a coffee for her. Stella offered David one of her sandwiches. The ice was broken, and things were back to normal. They discussed the last few days and Stella told David she was going to start back at yoga that night. Of course, David didn't mind Stella staying later to go to the Self Centre.

The afternoon passed all to quickly and soon David was saying goodnight and see her in the morning. Stella checked her emails before changing and walking over the road to the yoga studio. The class was a lovely Hatha Vitality class so lots of stretches and poses but no heat, just what was required, a gentle work back into it.

Sam was delighted to see her returned to class. "Where the hell have you been, lady?" she said jokingly.

Stella simply smiled and retorted, "Wouldn't you like to know?"

At that moment, Trudy appeared for the class. Shit, she had hoped that relationship was over, and really didn't want to have to justify herself to the society anymore. Trudy placed her yoga mat next to Stella's and gave her a hug, said "Hi," and began her pre-yoga stretching.

After, what was a difficult but invigorating hour, the class drew to a close. Trudy was on Stella like a shot. "I haven't seen you for a few weeks. Want a drink and a catch up?"

Stella had used the ten minutes of meditation time to think of a way out of this, she knew it was coming. "Ah Trudy, I would've loved to do that, but sadly I'm already meeting a drummer at the pub. We met a couple of weeks ago, he's lovely and I don't want to let him down. We must put something in the diary though. Give me a call with some dates." Inside, Stella was cracking up. Such a lie and one that would be round the society in no time.

"Oh, OK. Yes, I'll send you a text." Stella went to make small talk with Sam until she had given Trudy enough time to leave. She didn't want Trudy to see her ride off on her bicycle. Once enough time had passed, she left and went home.

Work the next day was mundane, with both Stella and David busy. It wasn't until she got home she realised she had a message from Trudy. It was great to see her, and did she fancy lunch one day next week. The drummer sounded dishy and she wanted to know all about him. "*I bet she did,*" Stella thought. Bloody nosey and wanted to spread more gossip with the society is all she was interested in. She couldn't meet her during the week as she was working. This was a little secret Stella needed to keep to herself, at least until the financial agreement had been reached.

That reminded her. She still had to respond to the solicitor's letter with the settlement offer. It was very tempting and certainly was enough to see her comfortable for the rest of her days. Tony had not disclosed how much he had by way of investments, nor pension, nor indeed anything else. He was hiding a lot more and she knew it. She would give it one last attempt to get an increase and if that happened, she would settle it. She would make a counter offer. One that was a bit crazy but let's see where it ends up. She would be no worse off as clearly Tony did not want to show her the extent of his hidden assets. She thought for a moment, poured a glass of wine to steel herself and wrote:

'Dear Sirs,

I thank you for your letter and I note the offer has been sensibly increased to something that was becoming more realistic. It is, however, rejected. Currently I have no idea of the extent of your client's wealth in terms of assets, shares, savings, investments and pension etc. built up over the course of our lengthy marriage. It would appear that your client is also reluctant to disclose his true worth. I am not wanting to prolong this, nor to make this any more painful than it needs to be. With that in mind, I am now giving a counter proposal. If agreed your client can keep his financial situation to himself. If it is not, I will require full disclosure going back a full twelve months from the date of our separation. With this disclosure I will do a full forensic accountancy audit in order to try and reveal the true position before deciding what I feel would be just in all the circumstances.

My proposals are as follows:

1. The home in which I reside is transferred to me outright;
2. The contents remain my absolute property;
3. A payment of £100,000 within 28 days of the order;
4. A further £100,000 in 18 months time;
5. A further £100,000 12 months thereafter; and
6. £300,000 pension transfer.

I am sure your client has more than one share purchase agreement and the second sum at number 5 is delayed to reflect the tax position once again for your client. I am trying to assist. The difference in our respective offers is only £150,000 and this is spread over some time. I hope your client will see the sense in this proposal.

Yours etc.'

Was she really this brazen? How would he react? Could she get away with that much? Tony would go mad when he read it. Sod him. Another mouthful of wine and the letter went into the envelope. She sealed it and placed it on the table to post the next day. Another mouthful. My god, how much had she changed in the last few months?

Chapter 16

On her way to work the next day, Stella stopped at the post box. She paused before putting the letter into the box. The solicitors would have to confront Tony with its contents the following day and once more, he had another ruined weekend to face. He would also probably be told by his mother that she was seeing a drummer, as that filtered round the society as well. It was not going to be a good weekend for Tony, she chuckled to herself. Serves him right.

As she cycled along, she wondered how difficult it would be to issue a divorce petition. Can't be that hard, can it? Maybe she would look into it today and see what could be done. That could ruin his next weekend too. Although she was loving life, even without her licence, she was still bitter and angry at Tony and what he had done. She needed to work that out of her system, but she knew it would take some time. He needed his comeuppance and the settlement would give her the satisfaction that, even though it may not be everything she could get, it would hurt him a lot. That would do for her.

Stella arrived first in the office for the first time that week, David would be impressed. She used the time to text Trudy and politely reject her invitation for lunch next week. She did not tell her why, of course. Trudy responded with a request for maybe a drink in the One Bull tomorrow night. Stella couldn't resist. Trudy was desperate to get more information. She went back to Trudy saying she had made plans to see a group at The Fox and was sorry. Nothing came back. Stella knew Trudy would put two and two together and come up with at least seventeen. She would be thinking that Stella was going to see her new man, the drummer, on Friday night at The Fox. Who in the society will appear at the Fox now, she wondered? In all probability, Trudy and her husband, she would want to keep it to herself until she had the proof and gossip for more points.

It was nearly time to open the office so Stella made David's coffee in anticipation of his arrival. He was appreciative. He looked tired. "Sorry Stella, been in the police station most of the night with a student rape case. Dreadful matter. Young university student at a party, very drunk, as was she. They were best mates until yesterday. Now she says he raped her as they slept together, never woke up but felt sore the next morning and he was still in bed. He's denying anything took place at all. He's being kept until they get the forensics back from the medical. They're fast tracking it and I'll probably be back there later today. Interesting case, from a legal point of view, if they charge him. Thanks for the coffee, I need it."

Stella told David to drink his coffee and go home to rest. There was nothing in court and she could cope without him. In truth, she had little to do and wanted to get online to investigate how to divorce someone. He agreed that home was a good place for him to be. He went, and said he would keep her posted and to ring if there were any issues.

Stella was straight on to the net. She googled divorce and was amazed at the range of online services she could access for essentially next to nothing. She signed up immediately and paid less than £100 for the forms all to be prepared. Stella had to input all the details: name, age, address etc. Address. She didn't actually know where Tony was living. Text Brian, he would know. She did and told him why. He was quick in his reply and yes, he knew it and now Stella had it. Great. The rest of the information was provided into the boxes including details of the adultery and the dates, how she found out and the date of separation.

The button was pressed and all the information was in the ether, winging its way to her cheapo divorce gurus who would prepare all the paperwork and get it back to her shortly. She also discovered that the government website would allow her to apply online. This was hilarious. She needed her marriage certificate though. That was at home, it would have to wait until at least tomorrow, depending on how quick the gurus were.

They were quick. Five minutes later she had an email. A draft petition and a step-by-step guide on what to do next. It also made reference to the government online service that she could use. Stella was feeling more excited by the minute. The rest of the day was spent not working at all and although she felt guilty about it, she couldn't help but dream and delight at the prospect of a divorce on her terms with financial security. Stella was happier than she had been in many years. Her life had passed her by, and now she was going to make up for all those lost and wasted years. All those years keeping house, raising Brian, looking after Tony. All of it at the expense of her own life. It was certainly changing, and more change was to come.

Stella was still on a high as she cycled home. The route took her past several fields with horses and pigs, The Fox and a few shops. It went past some other units and by now some of the occupants began to recognise her. They had started to acknowledge her, the odd smile or wave. Given the friendliness of the county they would soon be on speaking terms, with "morning" or "evening" being the call as she passed. Stella decided she would respond tonight with "Hi, I'm Stella," without breaking her stride on the pedals. The chance came quickly as the salesman (she assumed) at the Honda dealership called out, "Hi."

She replied with a smile and a "Hi, I'm Stella!"

And the response came shouted back, "Hi Stella, have a great evening, I'm Andy."

As she peddled on, she waved and replied "You too, Andy." What a lovely, almost surreal, moment the two strangers had shared.

A text arrived, it was from Lesley. "Hey, if the offer of a bed is still there, we would love to take you up on it."

Awesome. "Yes of course, how about some dinner first? How about you get here for seven and we take it from there? Any allergies?" Lesley replied in the affirmative, no allergies and now dinner was all on the cards.

Stella moved on to her divorce petition email and was determined tonight was the night to get the ball rolling. Carefully, she read through the draft petition for divorce prepared by the online gurus and recovered her original marriage certificate. All seemed perfect and in order. The government online issuing service was next, she wanted things underway. Like all government websites, you needed to register first, a painful experience of duplication and emails with links to confirm your identity etc. It took some time, but eventually it was done. Then the task of taking all the information from the guru's petition and copying it all over to the government one. Next, a scan of the marriage certificate. An insertion of her credit card details and hit submit. It was underway. Divorce petition without the need or help of Tony's solicitors. Stella felt very smug and relaxed back in the sofa with a celebratory glass of wine.

Work the next day went by in a flash and all Stella seemed

to be thinking about was the meal and company that night. She hadn't cooked for company in ages, but Lesley and Sam were easy going and fun, at least in the pub and, for Leslie, in the bedroom too. On the way home, she called in to the Co-op and bought some steaks from the butcher's counter, and some fresh salad and fruit. She would prepare a home-made pepper sauce and barbecue the steaks to serve with a side salad. For dessert, she would knock up a quick Eton mess, it seemed to be en vogue these days. She got home and worked to get all the preparation out of the way. Time was against her, so a quick shower was all she had time for.

Still in a towel when the doorbell rang, she answered to a stunned looking Sam, holding a bottle of wine. "I'm sorry," he stammered. "I didn't know it was that sort of meal."

Lesley gave him a quick backhand to the head and Stella apologised for her lack of clothing. In the kitchen she poured Sam and Leslie a large glass of red and said to Lesley, "Let me show you where your room is and I can get some clothes on too."

At the door to the spare room Stella managed to steal a hug and a passionate kiss with Leslie's hand reaching under the towel to caress a buttock. "Lovely," she said, "Its perfect." With a wicked wink she took off back downstairs to wait with her husband.

Once Stella got back downstairs, it was time to get things ready. Stella lit the barbecue and Sam offered to cook the steaks. They all sat outside chatting while the barbecue got up to temperature. There was discussion about the band, Flint Warriors apparently, and Stella told them the story about Trudy. She told them that Trudy would no doubt appear to check out the drummer of the band for herself. They thought this was awesome and were laughing far harder than she thought they ought to, until they told

Stella the band members were all mid-thirties! This was getting better and better.

With the food ready, they all went inside and enjoyed the steaks, beautifully cooked to order by Sam. They asked what Stella did for a living and she told them she worked for David Hughes, a criminal solicitor, she was his practice manager. Sam's face went bright red and Leslie choked on her mouthful of food. It was confession time for Sam. He told Stella, which she already knew from both the office file, having entered his case onto the computer, and Lesley, that the other week he was on a boy's night out, got worse for wear and was arrested. He had been asked to move by the police so he tried to do some body popping (he used to be quite good). His comment, "How do you like those moves?" was met with an arm in blue stopping him, the shove in return did not go down well. In fact, it got him a night in the cells at Martlesham police investigation centre. Once he had sobered up the next day he was extremely repentant, and given the hilarity of the situation and his lack of previous convictions, David managed to secure him a caution for his trouble. Stella laughed and told him not to worry, she was bound by confidentiality. Leslie was straight in, "You may be, but I'm not and he's still suffering, even now."

With that it was time to get down the pub before all the tables went. They walked down arm in arm and found The Fox starting to get busy. The girls found a table while Sam got the drinks in. The FWs, as it stated on the drum, were pretty much set up and the drummer was sitting in his seat showing off with his sticks. Stella took one look and there he was. No more than thirty-two, shaven head, bulging (in all the right places) T-shirt, bi-ceps of Charles Atlas, and a cheeky grin as he knew he was drop dead gorgeous. Leslie looked at Stella and they both fell on the floor laughing. Sam brought over four drinks, which for a moment, Stella found puzzling. He set the tray down, then he lifted a pint and headed straight to the drummer, whispering something in his ear before nodding in the girls' direction. There was no sign yet of Trudy or her husband.

The music started, and these boys were good. A little on the heavy side for Stella's taste but good none the less. By the third number, things were livening up and the dance area was starting to fill up nicely. Stella saw Trudy and her husband standing by the bar in the corner. Trudy was looking around but hadn't spotted Stella there. Leslie said, "Let's have a little dance," and the duo got to their feet and onto the floor. There was no way Trudy wouldn't know Stella was there now. The two danced away. In the interval before the next song the drummer picked up the mic.

"Before we do our next number, which is a bit slower and I know you all love it, I want to introduce you to someone special in the crowd. She's standing on the dance floor and she's about to get her first drumming lesson from me. Come on everyone, let's hear it for Stella!"

The crowd clapped and roared, and Lesley took Stella's arm and pulled her towards the drummer. There was nothing she could do, except go with it. This was priceless society stuff, and Tony would be furious, even though he had no right to be.

The drummer gave Stella a hug and sat her on his lap. OMG, this was amazing. He took her hands and placed a drumstick in each. Then he held each hand and said, "Relax, and let me do the work." The band started a slow bass riff and the drummer moved Stella's hands to the beat, only two drums but a nice rhythm. Then he whispered to Stella, "Keep this going, like this," and lifted his hands away and into the air. Stella was now drumming all by herself. The crowd loved it, even Trudy, who was staring and speechless. At the end of the demonstration the drummer gave Stella a kiss on the cheek and she thanked him. She returned to the table to huge applause and cheers. Stella was now a Fox celebrity.

Trudy was standing trying to hide herself and could not believe what she had just witnessed. This would keep the society going for weeks, and all the glory would be hers. Stella was seeing a new man, and what a man. Far younger than her, in fantastic shape and very good looking. She had to get away and hope that Stella hadn't noticed her.

Stella, meanwhile, was basking in the glory and the sheer fun and laughter of what had happened. It was just priceless. The trio of naughtiness continued to enjoy the band and there was much dancing and drinking. At some point Stella asked Sam how he had managed it. "It was simple," said Sam. "I bought him a pint and told him you had always wanted to learn the drums. He looked like a decent chap and he agreed, no problem. It went down really well, and I think they could use that more often. Nice little USP for them I reckon."

At the end of the evening, they all staggered back to Stella's. It really was such a long way back as they were in quite a state. A police car went by and Sam tried to look the other way. "No dancing please Sam," chuckled Stella. They all got in, and Stella made them all some toasted cheese sandwiches to soak up some of the alcohol and relieve them of the munchies they all seemed to have at that moment. It was enjoyed with a final glass of wine before they all retired to bed. While Sam was in the bathroom Lesley managed to find Stella's lips once more before everyone collapsed having had a truly memorable evening.

The next morning no one was alive before half ten, and it

was Stella who was downstairs first. She poured herself a huge glass of fresh orange to get some sugar into her and set about preparing breakfast for them all. Sam and Lesley came down looking as rough as Stella felt, but dressed and looking to leave. Stella refused to let them go as she had cooked breakfast, but more importantly, was not going to let either of them risk their driving licences until at least midday. As well she knew, it just wasn't worth it. So, the morning was spent with them all chilling in the front room, relaxing and trying to recover from the previous night.

They reminisced about last night, or the early bit, since that was all they could remember between them. Talk was around Trudy and how funny this false tale really was, how quickly the society would know, and what on earth they would be thinking about it all. Stella said that chances are they would already know, Trudy would have been on the phone to at least one of them first thing, if not last night. Trudy would also see them in town that morning, and no doubt enjoy telling the story over coffee in Café Nero.

Sam and Lesley left, but not before vowing to do something like this again soon. It had been a wonderful night, and they thanked Stella for putting them up. With the door shut and the house her own once again, Stella sat down, put her head back, closed her eyes and slept for another two hours.

Chapter 17

For once Stella had a quiet and relaxing weekend. The grocery order was delivered, and she managed to get all the house Hinched, which made her feel good. Stella settled herself down on the sofa and had a long conversation with Brian. He was fine, and his studies were going well. The new relationship was developing nicely, and he hoped to be home in a few weeks. He would stay with Stella and introduce the new girl to her, if that was OK. Stella looked forward to that and smiled at the thought of seeing them both. She confirmed her job was going well and told Brian about the divorce petition being issued and the fun she had last night. He was pleased she was doing well.

Stella had a long bath on Sunday and as usual, had some relaxing chill out music on with a glass of wine. She thought about the forthcoming events of next weekend and wondered what Julie would do? The prospect of a few days away left her feeling warm and excited making her giggle while she lay there. Tony would be furious about the settlement proposal, but she hadn't heard from him and also by now, no doubt, he would know about her new boyfriend, the drummer.

Monday came along far too quickly but as usual Stella rode to work. The weather was great, but the forecast was for rain the next day and heavy rain at that. As she rode to work, she wondered how she was going to cope in the rain cycling to work and back. She found herself looking at the sky and checking the clouds. It didn't look like rain anytime soon. '*Why did the weather have to change? It was perfect as it was.'* How would she stay dry? She needn't have worried though. When David arrived at the office, he was also aware of the forecast. He immediately spoke to Stella and said, "The weather doesn't look good for tomorrow. I've been thinking on the way in this morning. This is not a come on, but I don't want to see you in here looking like a drowned rat. Why don't you stay at mine tonight? I can cook. There is more than enough room and I would enjoy the company for a change."

Stella was surprised at the suggestion; sitting up straighter, she thought for several milliseconds before accepting the offer. She didn't want to cycle in the rain, she fancied David and she was single. She would want to keep it professional, but it would be nice to find out more about this kind, thoughtful and sexy boss of hers.

They got on with their respective work and chit-chatted through the day, each time Stella looked at him trying to hide her puppy dog eyes. Stella knew one of the rape cases was due to go back to the police station that day as they had released him, the forensics were simply taking too long. David checked, and it was confirmed he was to be charged and remanded when he returned to the station at six. David suggested they go to hers first, she could pick up a few bits and then they could call into the police station en route to David's house. It would only be a quick stop at the station and the boy, Bob Stocker, would be in court the next day. David just needed to get the forms for legal aid signed. The plan of action was agreed.

After work David duly gave Stella a lift home, after her bike was stored in the office kitchen, and he came in for a coffee while Stella threw some bits into a bag. In the bedroom, Stella was rushing between wardrobes and drawers frantically trying to find the right things, which in her panic made the job twice as hard. Eventually she managed to find everything she wanted and gave a huge sigh of relief. Once David had finished his coffee, they drove to the police investigation centre and arrived with ten minutes to spare. David was always prompt with clients; it made the right impression. He went into the station where, several months ago, Stella had been taken round the back way by the police. It brought back bad memories of that day. Another car pulled into the car park and a young lad got out from the passenger seat. He was thin, not bad looking, blonde hair and had a sad face. That must have been Bob. He walked into the station. Fifteen minutes later David came out alone. He went over to the other car and talked to the driver for a few minutes, shook his hand through the window and returned to Stella. Once they had left the car park, David confirmed Bob had been remanded for court the next day, but he was confident he would get bail in the morning. It was only a short drive across town until they pulled up at David's house.

This was the first time Stella had seen where David lived and it was impressive. Northgate Avenue was one of the best addresses in Bury. Old houses with big decent sized rooms, not overlooked or enclosed by the neighbours and good-sized gardens to the rear. They were rarely on the market and commanded a high price. She got out of the car and took a few moments to look at the front of the house, David's house, the porch in the middle straddled by two big bay windows, the lawn at the front – no bushes or plants, simply a herringbone footpath from front door to the gate. Stella was expecting the inside to be period furniture throughout, aga in the kitchen, old-style big radiators and a claw foot bath in the bathroom. She was so wrong. David had furnished it in a modern style and not at all the way she had pictured. David gave her a tour. The kitchen was big, with light oak units, a range cooker and lots of space, but also lots of things on the counter tops, although in nice neat rows. A big oak dining table was in the middle of the kitchen and was clear of everything. The dining room was being used as David's office. His desk sat so the chair backed towards the patio doors which led to the garden. Beneath it a large rug. His chair was a large leather chair and two leather club chairs sat on the opposite side of the desk. Qualifications were framed and on the walls with pictures from rugby matches interspersed, in contrast to the sparseness of his office at work. The front room was more comfortable, with a dark brown three-piece leather sofa and chairs, the only dark items in the room, and a large tv on the wall above the wood burner. There was a downstairs cloakroom, and upstairs a modern bathroom and four bedrooms. David showed Stella her room, not his, and then offered her a drink.

White wine in hand and back in the kitchen, David asked if chicken and mushroom pasta was OK.

"Sounds delicious." Stella sat at the kitchen table and watched David. She was surprised he could cook. The glass shook as her hand gently trembled when she raised it to her lips, the first sign that she was nervous to be here, alone, with David.

"Having been on my own for so long it was a must learn thing," he confided. She watched as he chopped the chicken thighs and fried them off in oil, garlic, pepper and a touch of cayenne. The mushrooms followed the chicken and they were left to sweat. Ciabatta was cut and drizzled with olive oil before going into the oven, and the fresh pasta went in another pan to boil. He also took some fresh basil roughly chopped it and grated some fresh Parmesan. Stella offered to help, but David wouldn't hear of it.

Once the food was on the table, David sat opposite Stella and offered her the chopped basil and Parmesan to add to her liking. He also told her she may want to season to taste, but not too much as the cayenne makes the dish and shouldn't be overpowered. *"Wow, impressive,"* she thought. The first mouthful was simply divine, he truly could cook, it wasn't all show! The smile on her face a clear sign that the food was indeed delicious. This man should not be single, where were his faults? She decided to ask him.

He replied with a shrug of his shoulders, "I don't know, that's for you to tell me. I used to work all the hours, but you know that. I am not into drugs, not controlling, not violent, don't drink to excess or use prostitutes. I'm just me. I get up, go to work and come home. I suppose I don't socialise much and that's probably why I'm single. I'm sort of used to it really."

After they had eaten, David offered desert and Stella declined, she was full and didn't want to spoil that. She offered to help with the washing-up, but the dishwasher did her out of that job. They retired to the living room. David put on some music, "Is jazz OK?"

"David, you are perfect, you are a gentleman, can cook, are a great boss and you like jazz."

David excused himself to go to the study and apply for Bob's legal aid online, leaving Stella to chill for a while with the jazz and the wine. Perfectly contented, she sat, holding the glass in both hands which rested on her lap and let the whole evening, the wine and the music wash over her, while once more taking in her new surroundings. David returned and they chatted about Bob's case. The forensic report was inconclusive, no semen showing but there was some DNA. That, David said, could potentially be argued away as they were in close contact, albeit not sexually.

After a bit more casual chat it was time to turn in. Stella said goodnight and went up to her room. David remained the perfect gentleman and bade her goodnight, but didn't try anything on. The bed was warm and comfortable, and Stella lay for a while thinking about David lying in the next room, wishing he wasn't and no doubt he was thinking the same.

In the morning, Stella washed, dressed and went downstairs. David had freshly brewed coffee and apple juice waiting with some toast and a variety of jams and marmalade to choose from. Stella was refreshed and enjoyed her breakfast, she told David as much. They went to the office and David headed off to deal with Bob at court. It was raining hard. Stella was glad she took David up on his offer. When he got back to the office the rain was even harder, bouncing off the road and big puddles were starting to form. Bob had been bailed and his case sent to Ipswich crown court for a preliminary hearing in four weeks' time. An email confirmed his legal aid had also been granted.

By the afternoon the downpour had come to an end and the sun was out drying the roads quickly. The puddles turning to steam and a heat haze rising from the sodden tarmac. Stella was able to cycle home. She didn't go to yoga; her gear was at home and in her haste yesterday she had forgotten to take it. Once home, she booked herself into the Thursday class instead. There was post waiting for her. A letter from Tony's solicitor.

'Dear Mrs Green,

We have spoken to our client and discussed the revised offer with him. We have advised him that the offer ought to be rejected, but against our advice he has chosen to accept it in full and final settlement.

We have also received an email from the online court system regarding divorce. This will not be contested. We have filed the appropriate form and include a copy for your records.

We note you are not using a solicitor and to assist we will prepare a draft consent order to deal with the financial aspects agreed above. We will forward this to you for approval within the next few days.

Yours etc.'

Well, that was a turn up. No doubt he had even more than she thought he did. Her cheeky letter has made her comfortable for the rest of her days and he still didn't know she was working. She hadn't anticipated it being so easy. Stella lay back on the sofa, held the letter up and read it again. She smiled and nodded in satisfaction. This weekend would now be an even better celebration with Julie.

The next couple of days went by without any excitement, even yoga on Thursday was peaceful, no Trudy. Andy at the garage was bright and cheery, and she looked forward to their brief exchanges, morning and evening. At the end of work on Friday, Stella said goodbye to David and cycled home. She had already packed the night before and it wasn't long before Julie turned up to collect her. They drove down the M11 to Epping and Stella could see Julie was nervous. It had to be said, Stella was excited at the prospect of spending the weekend with Julie and seeing what developed once they got to town. They used the time to catch up with each other's lives and ignored the elephant in the room.

They arrived at the flat at about seven thirty and it was beginning to get dark. The flat was as perfect as Stella had hoped, two double bedrooms with nice linens on the beds, her hand brushed them just to confirm it. A spacious lounge and separate small kitchen, tastefully decorated and simply ideal for the two nights they had. Both had a quick shower and refreshed themselves ready to explore the gay haunts of London and see what happens.

The Admiral Duncan was round the corner from where they were staying and as they approached, they saw the small terrace at the front of the pub. They looked at each other, Julie looked nervous as hell. Stella took her hand and squeezed it to try and relax her. "Let's go and have a drink. It'll settle the nerves and let's face it, we're here for a good time no matter what happens. Let's just have the attitude of, we're out for fun together, and relax a bit." Stella told Julie. She nodded in reply and they went inside.

It was dark but not dingy, seating around the walls leading to a long bar and a dance floor with a small stage at the back. It was fairly quiet with about forty or so others sitting around chatting. Stella bought two mojitos and they sat at an empty table. Both took a long mouthful of the cold cocktail, looked at each other, laughed and clinked the glasses together. Another mouthful, a smile and then Julie said to Stella, "Right let's get this party started."

Both of them chatted and observed. What is the etiquette for a place like this, they didn't want to cause offence? How does it work? They decided to watch. There were a few straight couples in and several girl-only couples and small groups, all seemingly sitting, laughing and chatting normally. Well, what did they expect? They were normal people after all.

A dark-haired lady walked in on her own, early 40s, tall, slim, fishnets and quite pretty. Julie watched her as she walked to the bar. She whispered to Stella, "She's quite pretty," and Stella chuckled. Julie continued to watch her at the bar and as the lady picked up her drink and turned round Julie looked away in embarrassment.

With a smile she walked over to the pair and looking straight at Julie said, "Do you mind if I join you? I am waiting for my friend to arrive and don't like sitting on my own, looks a bit sad I always think."

Stella answered for a tongue-tied Julie, "Yes, of course you can, I'm Stella and this is Julie, we're just in town for the weekend, for a bit of chill time."

"Hi Stella, hi Julie. I'm Amy. You can chill here OK, but it gets a bit lively in an hour or so. They have live drag acts which are fun. The girls come in and we all tend to have a good time. No trouble here, just drinks and giggles."

Julie spoke, "That sounds just what we are looking for and a drag act should be fun." The trio continued to chat amongst themselves and more drinks were bought. After about half an hour the pub was filling up and Amy's friend still had not shown up.

"Bloody Sandra," said Amy. "So unreliable, I'm getting really pissed off with her."

"Hey, just hang with us, you can make sure we don't get into any trouble," was Julie's response.

"Well, if you both don't mind that would be kinda cool. Are you two an item?"

Shit, now what to say? This was the first hint of their sexuality so far. Stella got in first, "No, we're not an item. We're good friends, have been for years. This is a new scene for us. As we said, we're here to chill and have a bit of fun."

Julie was, however, inspired by the mojitos. "Actually, Amy, what Stella said is true, but we were at Stella's a few weeks ago, got a bit tipsy and started talking, you know. We got round to talking about being with another woman and the thought turned me on. We're down here to see what happens, and if it does it cures a fantasy I have been having, if that makes sense."

Amy cracked up. "A closet lesbo with a bucket list. That's hilarious. Don't worry about it. Surely everyone has gay thoughts through their lives at some point, it's how you deal with it. There's no switch that says I like men or I like women, or even both. Everyone is an individual and mostly it happens naturally. I clocked you looking at me at the bar by the way and you are quite attractive. Tell me, have you never kissed a woman before? If not, this could be your first one?" With that Amy placed her hand on Julie's thigh and moved her face closer to Julie's.

Julie didn't move away and got as far as "No I have nev—" before Amy's mouth connected with Julie's and her spare hand cupped her face.

The kiss lasted several seconds before Amy broke away saying, "Well there you go, your first kiss with another woman. Now, how do you feel?"

Stella sat and watched, looking at Julie's reaction. Julie looked embarrassed as Stella was sitting beside her, "Oh my god!" she blurted out. "I was expecting to feel awful and dirty, but I don't, it was a kiss, and a kiss that has my tummy tingling."

"Well. it was my pleasure," replied Amy sitting back and removing her hand from Julie's thigh. She looked at Stella and said, "and how about you Stella, want to join the club?"

Stella leaned forward and gave Amy a kiss before saying, "Why the hell not?" They all laughed, and Julie relaxed at the sight of Stella joining and not leaving her feeling different.

The curtain on the stage twitched and out came the drag act. Cheers from the crowd and Supreme Stacey was on. They were a great act as well. The dance floor was soon full, and everyone was loving the act. Clapping and cheers from the crowd at the end of each song. The trio were also up and dancing. This weekend away was just what the doctor had ordered. It was, however, a little noisy for conversation and Stella asked Amy about She Soho round the corner. Amy confirmed it was a good club with a mixed age, but it was smaller and noisier than this one. She suggested the cocktail club in the village may suit them better.

It was clear to Stella that Julie was ready to embrace a woman and during the walk to the village, Julie took Amy's hand. It may well have been bravado brought on by the mojito's they had drunk, but so what, she was having fun. They walked along close to each other and, although she was delighted, Stella was beginning to feel like a bit of a gooseberry. The two were clearly getting on and there was no doubt in Stella's mind that Julie would have her first lesbian experience tonight. Once they arrived at the village and found the club, Amy went to the bar to get the drinks, and Stella looked at Julie. "You seem quite taken with Amy. Look, I know this is what this weekend is all about, but if you're uncomfortable about it or want to back out it's fine, don't do it just because you feel you have to. Do it because you want to."

Julie looked back at Stella, "Just don't leave me. Yes, I am fine with it and turned on by Amy, and would like to take her to bed for the experience, but don't abandon me and leave me all alone with her just yet. Can she stay at the flat with me? Is that OK?"

"Of course it is, if you're sure. I have no problem and you know it will always stay just between us."

Amy returned with the drinks and the three continued to chat. Amy was a nurse who worked in oncology, which was tough. She saw all sorts death and delight, and used the weekends to forget the pain she witnessed during the week. She had been a lesbian as long as she could remember and had never slept with a man, despite many offers. She had her own flat which she rented in Stratford, just her and her pet cat who came and went as he pleased. He was the only man in her life. The cocktail bar was much quieter, which made talking much easier, no need to shout. During the next hour or so several others came and went, Amy's friends all stopping to say hi to Amy and to be properly introduced to Stella and Julie. It was a very pleasurable evening, and Julie and Amy were certainly getting on well. They were both touching and stroking each other's thighs and faces, all perfectly normal for this place, although it was odd for Stella to see Julie doing it, but she didn't mind at all.

It was nearer one than twelve before they left, and Julie had invited Amy back to the flat to spend the night. Stella was drunk and exhausted, the other two were drunk, exhausted and horny. Once they got back to the flat Stella gave them both a kiss and a hug and said her goodnights and left them to it. She climbed into bed, and heard and saw nothing until she woke the next morning, late. The other two were nowhere to be seen, although shoes were still discarded in the hallway. Stella made the coffee and the sound of the kettle must have roused them. Amy came through first, still doing up the buttons on her blouse and tucking it into her jeans. "I think Julie enjoyed herself," was her opening comment.

When Julie followed, she had overheard Amy's comment and simply said, "Very much." After coffee Amy said her goodbyes and had to go home to check the cat was OK.

Once Stella and Julie were ready, they decided to hit Westfield for some retail therapy. Nothing was said about the previous night, and the pair went round a number of shops, trying on dresses, blouses, skirts etc. They both found themselves new outfits and sat down in a nearby hotel for some afternoon tea. They both needed sustenance and a sugar fix.

It was at this point Stella looked at Julie and simply said, "Come on, now Amy has gone you can be honest with me. How was it for you?"

Julie was sheepish, this was Stella and until last night they were both straight, or so she thought. What would Stella think of her? Julie confirmed her night with Amy was enlightening and wonderful, she loved the things that she did and that Amy did to her, the feel of another woman's breasts against her own and to touch another woman. She would like to experience more, but didn't want her husband to know about it. Did Stella think any differently towards her for doing it?

Stella decided it was time to come clean. She confided in Julie and told her about Lesley and how she felt too. She confirmed she shared the same feelings Julie was feeling, which is why she hadn't told Julie before. Julie understood and was greatly relieved that nothing had changed in their relationship. Julie told Stella that Amy had given her number to her and said she would like to see her again. That night though, they would try She Soho and see how they got on.

They returned to the flat and got ready for the next night of fun. Both put on their new outfits and both looked amazing, and younger or trendier in them than their other clothes. They went out and found an Italian nearby and had a light meal before venturing to She Soho.

It was a basement establishment, smaller and cosier than last night's venues, still with a pleasant but more erotic atmosphere than yesterdays. Stella went all out and bought a bottle of champagne for them to celebrate Julie's new found lust for life and all things feminine. They sat against the wall, watching the crowd, the place was busy. They sat close, shoulder to shoulder relishing the champagne and admiring the clientele. Both saw ladies they liked the look of, but no one, it seemed, was paying them any interest. The music started, and they got up to dance. It was a bit garage and not their scene but they had a dance together anyway. Stella felt a hand on her bum, it was rubbing and squeezing gently. She turned to look and saw a much younger girl, who didn't remove her hand, just let it linger so it was now on her thigh. This girl was attractive, but also only in her 20s. Stella smiled and put her arms over her shoulders to dance with her. The youngster lent in and told Stella she was Kate and had been looking at her for a while, found her very attractive, before kissing her on the neck. The champagne and the erotic atmosphere got the better of Stella and she moved her head round and kissed her on the mouth, open mouthed and tongues entwined.

Julie could only see from the back, but watched Kate pull Stella in close. She knew Stella had pulled. She continued to dance and soon caught the eye of another lady and before long they too were enjoying themselves on the dance floor. This new found four spent the evening together, but really as two separate pairs. This place was certainly more full-on than The Admiral and it was getting quite steamy, reminding Stella of her school discos where the boys would take you to a quiet corner for a snog and a grope. It was fun, but Stella didn't want that sort of sex with either a woman or a man. She was older and had more respect for herself. Kate did try to take things further by putting her hand up Stella's skirt and rubbing her through her knickers. Stella took Kate's hand away, she was not up for a public showing. Stella could see that Julie was in a similar but slightly less awkward situation. Kate took the hint and said she needed the loo. She did not return, instead, no doubt, off to find someone a little looser than Stella wanted to be. Julie and Stella left the club and were thinking about going back to Village but decided to call it a night and grabbed a bottle of wine from an off-licence before going back to the flat.

They sat on the sofa together and drank wine. Legs entwined both tipsy and horny. They did stroke each other's thighs but it was more playful than sexual. They had now both tasted woman, both enjoyed it, but were not prepared to risk their friendship over it. Instead, they chatted more about the day and evening they'd had. Both being honest about their feelings for both men and women and both saying they should make this a regular trip for them to escape the mundane world of safe Suffolk.

It was time for them to return home. They waited until late afternoon, using a leisurely walk along the embankment to clear their heads, and made sure Julie was safe to drive, before hitting the tube to Epping and the car journey home. Both had had a wonderful, exciting, hectic but refreshing weekend and both wanted to get home, relax in the bath and sleep in readiness for work the next day.

Chapter 18

Once Julie had got Stella back home safely, Stella asked her if she wanted to come in for a coffee. It was bucketing down outside, and the journey had been horrendous. Julie needed five minutes before her drive home, so she readily accepted the kind offer. The pair ran from the car trying desperately to prevent their hair getting wet in the near monsoon. It was of course futile, and the hair was drenched and in need of a towel dry before anything else could be done. Stella made the drinks and they both sat in the kitchen, tired heads nursing the coffee, one hand resting on damp hair. Even though they were both exhausted and hungover Stella could feel an electric atmosphere, high with sexual tension. After the coffee was finished, Julie said she needed to get home. They hugged at the door and instinctively both kissed the other on the mouth, but rather than the normal friendly kiss on the cheek they had got used to, this kiss only intensified the sexual tension in the air. They parted and both looking a little flushed, not knowing if with desire or embarrassment, they said nothing and Julie left to go home.

  Stella took her things upstairs and ran a much-needed bath. Tonight it was bath salts and bubble bath, what the hell, she knew how to live. She chuckled to herself. No wine tonight, Stella needed to sleep, and alcohol would not help her achieve that aim. She put the TV on in the bedroom to catch the evening news and sank deep into the bath. She closed her eyes and half-listened to the news, half thought about the weekend and Julie, then Lesley and lastly David. The last few months had turned her world inside out and upside down, and now she had new problems to cope with. She had sorted her finances out and started the divorce, but now she had a female playmate, and two other potential dalliances in Julie and David. What to do?

She got out of the bath and went straight to bed, too tired even for dinner and, to be fair, she wasn't that hungry. The pair had eaten well and badly over the weekend and she needed to get back to a proper low-carb, high protein diet to complement her yoga and her move towards fitness once more. The phone rang and in her semi-conscious state she answered. It was David. Had she seen the weather forecast? It was going to remain wet for most of next week. He wasn't going to take no for an answer, she was to pack some things and stay with him until the storm had gone, probably until Thursday at least. It wasn't until after the call she realised what she had agreed to. Staying with her boss was fine, but knowing that they both lusted after each other was another thing. She put her head on the pillow and even though it had not yet reached eight p.m. she slept, solidly.

The alarm woke her and she remembered last night's conversation. She grabbed a bag and packed a week's worth of work clothes, gym gear, something to change into for the evenings, decent underwear, bare essentials make up, and thought she had enough to cope. She made her breakfast and was ready when David arrived at 8.40 a.m. to take her to the office.

"Are you sure about this?" she enquired after the pleasantries.

"Yes, of course, I wouldn't have offered if I wasn't. You survived one night and weren't too unruly as a house guest. We can share the cooking if you like, and we can discuss the way forward with the business. You've impressed me at work greatly."

The day was busy with loads of banking to catch up on, it was nearing time for the VAT return. There had been a legal aid payment over the weekend which meant Stella had loads of reconciliation work to do. Thankfully, it also enhanced the cash flow. David had been on duty at the police station as well, so there was all of that work to do. It wasn't all going to get done today, she thought, although she hated leaving work still to do at the end of the day.

David, for his part, had been out in court all day. A number of regular clients found themselves up before the various benches and District Judge that day. A few guilty pleas, some trials to be fixed and a sentencing to do. Most of it meant that work could be billed, so it would be a great start to the next legal aid return. Work at the practice was going well, increasing as David had much more time available, now he had Stella on board. By half past three he was finished at court. He drove back to the office arriving at about an hour later. He told Stella she should finish what she was doing and be ready to go in ten minutes, she had clearly worked hard enough judging by the way the paper had moved from her desk. He rang one of his police station agents and asked him to cover for the week since he had guests staying. That was no problem, and all agreed. David's phone wouldn't even ring, he could turn it off, something he had not done for at least five years.

He chased Stella out of her office and drove her straight to his home. They walked in and Stella was shown to the same bedroom she had used the previous week. Stella dumped her bag and returned downstairs to find David opening a bottle of red, a nice Shiraz by the look of it.

"This should go well with the beef I have planned for

tonight. Do you approve?"

Such a gentleman. "Yes, of course. How can I help?"

David responded with, "You can help by sitting at the kitchen table and keeping me company."

Stella was uncomfortable with this, after all, she was a guest for a few days and wasn't used to anyone else ever looking after her in this way, but she didn't argue. She sat as she was told and watched David cook for her, gently holding her wine, eyes on him at all times. She was smiling.

David got on with preparing a small beef joint, adding some red wine and baby onions to the tray for good measure. There were carrots and dauphinois potatoes also being prepared. Stella sat, fascinated by the skills of her boss as a cook, despite what he said to her last time, she really did not expect a proper cook to add to all the other positives he held to her.

With everything in the oven, David joined Stella at the kitchen table, sitting opposite and placing the wine bottle on the table after topping Stella and himself up.

"Now Stella, please relax. As a house guest you're OK. There were no problems last week, in fact, I rather enjoyed the company. Please make yourself at home for the next few days. Help yourself to the food, the wine and the bath. You don't need to ask, just do whatever you feel you want to."

"*If only,*" went straight to the front of Stella's mind. "Thanks David, I will try, but I really do need to help you out. I have never been waited on like this before, and it's a bit alien to me."

"OK, well the cutlery, placemats, and napkins and over there, there, and there. If it would make you feel better, you can set the table for dinner."

"Yes, it would."

Stella rose and went to the various places in the kitchen

discovering cutlery, napkins and placemats. She set her own place first and then walked round behind David to set his place. As she leant over, she was forced to push her breasts up against David's back, she liked the feel of them up close to him. She could smell him too, no aftershave just the smell of man. It felt and smelt good. David didn't move, or flinch and Stella returned to her seat. There was the sound of an alarm, and David got up. "That'll be the dinner ready then." He went to the oven and served up the meal. It was delicious, every morsel.

After they had eaten, Stella helped David load the dishwasher and they retired to the sitting room. David put some music on, remembering Stella was partial to jazz. He opened the conversation about the business. He told her that since she had started, things had improved greatly. He knew that she would be a bonus to the firm but didn't appreciate quite how good she was. The books were up to date and the bank was looking very healthy. He had more time to deal with clients and increase the number of cases he was working on. He could see profits going up and this was all down to Stella, well in his head anyway.

Stella reminded him these things were looking better due to the fact that things were getting billed on time and more accurately. The healthy balance in the office account was not to be taken as read. The money in it included the VAT which was due to be paid out shortly, and this would take a big chunk of the balance away. He had enough money to cover it and the expenses, but it was a bit tight. She suggested he open a separate account just for the VAT and that would leave the office account with a much truer picture. David thought that a great idea and he would get a new account opened as soon as he could. He also told Stella that he was looking at taking on another solicitor. His reasoning was simple, he wanted someone who would grow with the business in order that when he retired, he could sell it to them as a going concern, rather than let it simply close and be worthless. It would also help keep his clients with decent representation.

Stella said he shouldn't rush into it but should cost it and add it to his business plan, which needed updating anyway. She would look at the figures and see how best to do it. David was pleased she felt able to challenge him in this way. Stella asked if she could have a bath before bed and David repeated that she should treat the house as her own and of course she could. It was her bathroom, he had an en-suite off his bedroom, so wouldn't need to use the main one. With that, they said goodnight and Stella went up the stairs. She had her bath and left the bathroom door unlocked, not believing David would intrude, he didn't.

The next day the rain continued to pour and David was in the office. There was a training day at court, so no courts were sitting except the overnight remands, which David didn't have. Stella decided to get straight on with her new priority of the business plan. She had to ask David a few questions about what he was looking for in a new solicitor, salary etc, how you get to be a duty solicitor and David answered all her questions. He was feeling far less stressed with the job these days and the office atmosphere was lovely and relaxed with Stella about. The new and updated business plan was coming along a storm when David announced it was time to go home. She hadn't realised the time; this was the sort of thing she loved doing and all her old experience came flooding back to her.

They got back to Davids and had to run inside the porch to get away from the rain. Stella swore it was getting worse. They went inside and both went to the kitchen. David got the wine and Stella the glasses. David poured. "Tonight's masterpiece," David announced, "Is tacos! Every so often it doesn't hurt to get messy food and to chill right down."

Stella was most surprised and didn't expect David to chill out with tacos, but it was a great idea. Stella made the guacamole while David prepared the chilli mince. A tomato salsa and chopped lettuce were soon put together and the pre-bought shells went into the oven to warm. They continued to sit at the kitchen table and chatted while eating messy food together.

As they started to clear away, David took the bowls to the dishwasher, rinsed them before placing them neatly inside. Stella had the plates and they were rinsed. She walked over to David who was bending over the dishwasher to hand him the plates, as she did so David rose and turned to face Stella. The timing was perfect, they were face to face barely a fingers width apart. The tension rose and David simply said, "May I?"

There was no hesitation in Stella's voice, "You may."

David took his free hand and gently cupped her face; he moved his mouth to hers and their lips met. The kiss was long and lingering, and neither wanted to relinquish the others lips. David embraced Stella who allowed it to happen while she still had a plate in each hand. The hug was tight, and the kiss continued. Eventually it was David that broke the hold, he stepped back nearly falling into the dishwasher, took the plates and placed them where they belonged.

"I am so sorr—" he started to say.

"Don't be," she interrupted. "Look David, this has been building probably since the first coffee. I know you shouldn't see staff and I know how it could look. Hell, it ruined my marriage, but we're both single. This isn't office time, and we are both consenting adults. If you're OK with it, let's just go to bed."

David closed the dishwasher door and took Stella by the hand, saying nothing. He led her upstairs and into his bedroom.

The room was large with a king size sleigh bed at one end. Modern, matching furniture, nothing on the walls except for a television. He took her to the end of the bed, turned her to face him and once more took her face in his hands. This time the kiss was more passionate, more forceful, more necessary. Stella held him tight and kissed back, urgently. The embrace lasted for several minutes before David lowered Stella onto the bed, HIS bed. This was the moment Stella had dreamt about. This was the moment she had imagined in the bath. He lay beside her just looking for a moment. "You are very beautiful," the words fell effortlessly from his lips. He reached a hand to her waist, placing the other behind her head. He leant in to her and they kissed some more. Tongues embracing each other as the lust rose inside them. His hand moved to her stomach, gently touching before ascending to find her breast. He engulfed it as much as he could with his hand and squeezed gently forcing a sigh to leave Stella's open mouth. A sigh that left her mouth and entered his. Stella reached round to stroke his waist.

His hand continued to entice her breast, pleading for her nipple to swell while safe within the bra and blouse, before he reached for the buttons of the blouse and started to release her. Stella was now feeling his chest, a hand inside the shirt tenderly stroking over his own nipple, she removed it and lay back to allow David better access to her buttons. He opened the blouse and his eyes became wide when he gazed upon the fullness of her breasts before him. A front opening clasp was soon undone and her breasts were finally exposed to him, nipples so very erect and begging to be suckled and teased. He obliged and placed his mouth over her nipple, wide open, using his tongue to entice it further before placing it gently between his teeth and continuing his skilful taunting with his tongue.

Stella could well have climaxed just by the way he was exciting her nipple, the tongue on one and fingers deftly encouraging the other. She reached down and stroked his thigh, her hand rising up until she could feel the swelling between his legs. She caressed, he caressed. The excitement rose up. She pushed David away and onto his back. She was now in control. She unbuttoned his shirt and undid his trousers. She stood at the end of the bed and pulled his trousers and pants down releasing him. He was very hard. She climbed back on top of David, choosing to ignore his erect penis and kissed his chest all over, saving his nipples until last where she lingered. As she took the first one into her mouth his back arched in pleasure, and again when her fingers squeezed the lonely one. Again, and higher when she bit down on it, hers was not soft and gentle but hard and demanding. She moved her mouth down enjoying his tummy and then his inner thigh, down to the knee and back up the other side. She was between his legs; he was at her mercy. She licked the base of his penis before slowly moving up, up to the tip, tasting him for the first time. She toyed with him feeling him throb, arching his back, desperate to be engulfed in her warm mouth. He didn't have to wait too long, Stella wanted it as much as he did. She took him deep inside her mouth.

It was the first time in a long time for both of them. He was nearing a climax; he took her head from him. "No, I want to be inside you. I want to explode inside you. It's been so long I am not sure how much longer I can last." He moved her onto her back and placed his hand on her knee. He ran it up her thigh, feeling Stella tense slightly as he did so. He felt her pants. They were already damp. He eased them off, discarding them recklessly on the floor. His fingers returned and massaged, outside, then stroking the length of her vagina before finding the little mound at the top, already hot and erect. Stella moaned again as he rubbed and massaged before he placed his fingers inside, using them urgently.

A climax flew through Stella's body as she quivered beneath him. He turned her over onto her tummy. He spread her legs wide and raised her off the bed to allow himself the access they both desired. He found her entrance and used his knees to spread her wider. His hands were on her back, pushing her down into the bed. He was going to have her right there, right now. His thrusts were hard and deep, his hands firmly keeping her in place. My god this was good, hard and dominant. Stella came again. The wave of her orgasm was simply too much for David, moments later he exploded deep inside her, pumping himself again and again until he was spent.

The first time is always memorable but never the best sex. He collapsed on top of her and she breathed a sigh of contentment. Stella felt comfort in the fact that, at last, she had had sex with a man again, but not any man, not a random night-club one-off, no, sex with David.

They lay in each other's arms for a few minutes contemplating what had happened. David feeling both embarrassed and euphoric at the same time, Stella feeling satiated and satisfied. David spoke first, "That should not have happened, and I apologise now. If you want to leave, I will run you home. If you don't want to work for me, we can work something out there too."

Stella's response was immediate, "It should have, did, and was wonderful. It makes the office a little trickier, but we are not teenagers and we can keep work professional. I don't want a full-blown relationship at the moment, but if I did, one with you would be fantastic. I'm still getting over my marriage. Let's play it by ear, be grown-ups and see how we both feel after my holiday." That seemed to relax David, who was no doubt worried about his professional standing after this and how it would look to the profession outside.

They spent the next two days and nights together, Stella remained at David's even though the rain had stopped by Thursday. While at David's they cooked together, relaxed together, chatted and made love several more times, each time better than the last for both of them. At work, things were normal, the atmosphere was even lighter now the sexual tension was gone, and both behaved like real adults going about their work and enjoying it.

By Friday, Stella had almost put the finishing touches to the business plan. She had a meeting with David in the afternoon and took him through it.

He was impressed with both the quality of it and the speed with which it was delivered. It seemed Stella had done projections on fee income based on two-thirds of the level of duty work David alone generated, taken from the last twelve months. The figures stacked up nicely. There was space in the office, but the outlay needed to bring in another lawyer and the timing needed to be considered further. It seemed the best time was a month before the new duty solicitor rota came out later in the summer. This gave them time to find the right person, which, given the current funding on legal aid, was no easy task. They discussed bringing in someone perhaps with higher rights of audience so they could have the added benefit of crown court income. They would see who was best suited to the role as a whole and decide. David was keen to use Stella and her experience in this process as she had proved to be invaluable so far. The one thing Stella hadn't covered, David noted, was her own role, which was now far beyond what it was supposed to be.

At the end of the meeting, they decided to call it a day at three thirty, and Stella told David she needed to go home to sort her place out. She thanked him for putting her up for the last few days, but she had things she needed to attend to. David understood and dropped her home, not even asking for an invitation to come inside.

Chapter 19

Stella picked up the post and poured a glass of wine. She sat in the lounge and started to open the mail. It was mostly junk which she swiftly discarded onto the coffee table. There was a card from her son, which was a catch up and miss you type of card. All was well in his world and his new relationship was blossoming. Stella couldn't wait to meet her, she sounded really good for him and Stella was pleased. She would call Brian over the weekend for a proper chat. The bank statement was in, and her balance was looking healthy. The new job and not driving was certainly a cost-saving scheme, a ban had its benefits (especially the last few days) but not really a selling point for drinking and driving. There was also a draft consent order from Tony's solicitors. Stella read it and it seemed fine. Stella grabbed the bull by the horns and went straight online, she logged onto her court page and inputting all the details for the financial agreement to be considered. She scanned the draft order and the letter from Tony's solicitor for completeness and pressed upload. Now it was wait and see. Sadly, there were some missed delivery items the Royal Mail had at the sorting office for her to collect, maybe Lesley could help.

She picked up her phone and sent her a text.

'Be awfully nice for a catch up and I could do with a lift to the sorting office at Morton Hall to collect some parcels if you're about. S x'

The reply was swift,

'Sam has gone off for the weekend, we had a bit of a set to

and I could do with a friendly hug. If you're up for it, I can come over and take you to get your bits Lx'

It was agreed Lesley would be over in the next half hour to run her to the sorting office. While waiting Stella went through her emails, in her David distraction she had not kept an eye on those for a few days. There was an email from the online divorce court, they had all the paperwork and a date would be set for the decree nisi to be pronounced, Stella was a bit taken aback by that, all those years of marriage would soon be confined to room 101 and all by email. She felt a little sad at the waste, but knew this was the right way forward without a doubt.

Lesley turned up with a bottle of wine and a kiss for Stella, it seemed so natural now that the response was mutual. Together, they went to the sorting office and collected her parcels. It was the camera and most of the safari gear as she had thought. Stella was excited about opening them.

They got back to Stella's and Lesley said she hoped Stella didn't mind about the wine as she needed a drink and could think of no better place to share it. Stella was, of course, fine with that and she pulled out some pizza from the freezer to heat up. While the pizza was warming, Stella started opening the packages, lots of clothes and the camera. She was a good photographer and was soon happy everything was in order. While she was looking at the camera, she hadn't noticed Lesley who had stripped off and was busy trying on Stella's new clothes. Stella took the opportunity to try out the camera for real, using Lesley as her model. Lesley was good as a model, she knew how to pose and now they were on their second bottle of wine, the poses became more raunchy, buttons were being undone and breasts partially exposed. The pictures were mildly erotic, not pornographic, and given the lighting, were pretty good. Lesley convinced Stella to try the clothes on too, and Lesley took some shots of Stella, it was all very risqué. The shots became topless and they practiced with the timer for some shots of the two of them together. It was becoming steamy.

All of a sudden, there was a knock at the door and then a face appeared at the window. It was Tony! He would have seen Stella and Lesley cavorting for the camera through the front room window. Stella quickly grabbed a safari shirt and pulled it on before going to the door.

"What the fuck are you doing peering through my window?" she said with more than a little force in her voice to try and diffuse the embarrassment.

"I could ask what you were doing," came the response, "but I don't think I need to. I saw a car and wondered who it was. Look Stella, I don't want to row, I wanted to talk to you like adults, but I can see you are busy, I can come back."

Lesley came into the hall, still topless, put her arm round Stella's shoulder and said, "Yes we are busy, busy and tipsy, so piss off before we report the peeping tom to the old bill."

Stella said, "This is just a friend and we are playing with my new camera and clothes. Come back Sunday afternoon if you have to." And with that she closed the door.

Giggling the pair returned to the lounge still with Lesley's arm draped over Stella's shoulder, and Stella then went to refill the glasses and get the pizza. When she returned, Lesley asked who that was. Stella filled her in on all the gory details of her past and brought her right up to speed. Stella knew this would get round the society with some lesbian spin attached to it, which was not good for such a conservative town and the ultra-conservative society members darling! Frankly though, she didn't care much. That was her former life and inside, those ladies what lunch, would be jealous as hell that she had broken away from a cheating husband and was actually doing all right at the same time.

Stella invited Lesley to join her in a bath, and they did so with more wine, after tidying up the dinner (for want of any other word for it, it was hardly dinner.) Both lay in the bath and the bubbles with their wine, legs entwined and relaxed.

Lesley used the opportunity to tell her about the argument with Sam. Essentially, she had over-spent and money was getting tight. They had a huge row about it and Sam had run off to his mothers on Wednesday. His job was not very secure at the moment and he was worried. Lesley had over-reacted as usual and she missed him. She knew it was her fault but wasn't going to back down just yet, not while he was with his mother. The pair had never seen eye to eye.

After the bath they climbed into Stella's bed and cuddled. Stella put a film on the TV and together they snuggled, chatted away and watched the film. This night was not sexually charged and lying there with Lesley in her arms now felt as natural to her as it would have done if it had been David. It was a truly gentle, loving friendship that had developed from lust and experimentation. Stella was becoming comfortable with her new-found sexuality. At the end of the day, it was just a body, just skin with two minds that got on and understood each other, gender had become unimportant.

By the time the film had finished, Lesley was asleep in Stella's arms, mentally exhausted from her domestic problems, physically tired from the camera cavorting and totally relaxed in bed. Stella leant over and gave her a kiss on the cheek and cuddled down with her for the night.

The next morning, Lesley and Stella had a lazy lie in with

coffee in bed. It had been a lovely evening and neither particularly wanted it to end. Their friendship was developing far beyond that of casual sex. Between them they decided to spend the day together, mooching around in Cambridge. Stella hadn't been there for so long, she was sure she was bound to be spotted, but it was out now anyway. So really, what the hell? Lesley simply wanted the company and to not return to an empty house.

They parked at Newmarket road park-and-ride and rode the bus into town. Neither had done this before, but the Grafton parking charges were expensive now, and, given the recent turns in their fortunes, it seemed a more necessary and obvious choice. Sitting together on the bus and chatting, Lesley slipped her hand into Stella's and Stella squeezed it. It was all very natural, loving, friendly and well, it seemed like the normal thing to do, as they watched the passers-by while the bus trundled on. They got off at the Grafton centre and walked over the parks into town. It was a lovely walk in the sun, with just the odd bicycle to dodge and the occasional waft of cannabis to cope with. They window-shopped in Red Lion Yard, resisting the temptation of John Lewis, and sat for coffee and pastries in a quaint coffee shop in one of the many side streets. All the while the conversation flowed, nothing in particular just part of the passage of learning for each of them about the other.

They walked round the market square and made their way towards the river. Both enjoyed walking hand in hand admiring the architecture and watching the world dash by, desperate to get the shopping done or get to the library, or home. It was a fabulous day. They walked down the river towpath away from the town centre, watching young love on the grass, families and couples in punts and kids playing football. This is how life should be, Stella mused as they walked on. Soon they had done a full circle and found themselves only a short walk from the Grafton Centre once more. They found a pub nearby and stopped for a bite to eat and a glass of pinot grigio to wash it down, before catching the bus back to the car and back to Stella's.

Stella invited Lesley in, but she declined stating that she didn't want to overstay her welcome, she'd had a great day and wanted to meet up again soon. Stella agreed that their time together had been wonderful and said that she would keep in touch. The evening was spent reconsidering the new clothing and checking the pictures taken yesterday. A sigh escaped from her and she looked on the small screen remembering the previous evening and wondering what David would make of it if he found out. He had sent a text earlier inviting Stella round, but she declined, indicating that she had her personal paperwork to get through even though she would love to have seen him.

Her holiday was now only a few weeks away, so she spent the solitude checking and double checking. Making a list of everything that was needed and going through the list, ticking what was done and wondering about what was left to do. She started in one of the spare bedrooms, laying out the clothes she was going to take with her and making little piles for packing at a later date. She was making sure that she was fully prepared for this solo adventure. Never before had she been away on her own like this and the thought was both exciting and made her nervous to.

The next morning, Stella was up bright and early and spent the time alone catching up on housework. She had neglected her cleaning and washing duties, and she attacked the house with a new-found energy that she hadn't felt for a long time. Life for her was certainly improving and she could see a wonderful future ahead. It was to be a life of contentment and adventure, no pressure from partners. Who she would be with ultimately, she did not know? David may not approve of her bi-sexuality or she may give it up for a life with him, she didn't know and right now, it wasn't important. It was for the future and, given recent events, she had no idea what that future held, she just knew she was looking forward to it. Once she finished the cleaning, she sat down on a bar stool for a break, it was the afternoon, just, so it was wine o'clock and a cold white Chablis was in order. Glass poured, she relaxed. She then remembered Tony was coming round. What did he want? Well, she would find out soon enough she supposed.

It was an hour or so later when there was a knock at the door. Stella knew it was Tony, she opened the door and he stepped in sheepishly.

"Can I come in please? We need to talk," Was his feeble opening line. Stella gestured with her head for him to come through.

She led him to the kitchen and offered him a seat, poured herself a glass of wine and said, "You mean you need to talk. I don't need to talk at all, thanks. What do you want?" Stella was not going to let him an easy ride, whatever it was.

He started with an apology for turning up unannounced on Friday evening and said what she did was her business, not his and it would go no further, on his honour.

Stella was straight back. "Your honour, what honour do you have to give? You screwed around in our marriage and would still be doing so if I hadn't caught you out. You try to make out you're skint to your lawyers and treat me like a fool, when I am far from one, you have no honour left at all. As for Friday, you're right, you have no idea what was going on and nor will I tell you, it's simply not your concern. All I want is for this divorce to complete and for you to be out of my life, so I can get on with it in peace."

"Listen to me, please, Stella. We need to at least be civil. We have a son," Was his response.

"Yes, we do, a son that cannot even speak to you, let alone see you for what you have done, and I don't blame him. Don't make him your excuse, now what do you want?"

"OK, OK, but will you hear me out to the very end, please Stella, please?"

Stella remained silent and took a mouthful of wine, all the time watching for any facial give away.

"I accept I have treated you badly, I have torn up our wedding vows and any trust you had for me. I have ignored your love and hard work that you put into the house and yes, I thought I might get away lightly financially through the divorce. I also thought Brian would understand that things happen between people and not take sides. I thought I was in love with Sue, and that we would be perfect together, just like when we first got together. The perfect couple we were, and I miss that.

I have made mistakes and the biggest one was leaving you. I am still in love with you Stella and I really want to try and get us back on track. I'll do anything you want to fix the situation. Please give me a chance to at least show you how much you mean to me?"

Where the hell was this coming from? He wants another go? To fix things? Why? What's his agenda?

So, she asked, scathing not enquiring, her mouth showing she was angry, "Why? What's happened? What's changed?"

"Well, it's sort of complicated really – several things. Firstly, there is Brian, I love my son and want to be a real dad to him, help him through uni, watch him grow up, marry, have his own kids. These are important to me. Second, there is Sue. She's OK, but not the brightest, and although I thought we could make a go of it, living together simply isn't going to work. We are from different generations, different tastes, expectations. Hell, she can't even cook. You spoiled me there. She's becoming dull and high-maintenance, and with this settlement I agreed to, it's taking its toll. I can't cope. I got to thinking and really, I want things back to how they were before, just us, the perfect couple again. What do you say, Stella?"

Stella was dumbstruck for a moment. He wanted her back so he could have a relationship with his son, save money and get looked after by someone his own age? That's essentially what he was saying, wasn't it? She could barely believe he had the audacity to even suggest a reconciliation with that little speech.

Stella came back at him, her voice raised, her heckles were up, "That has to be probably the worst 'I want you back' speech ever. You don't want me back at all. What you want is your old life and the easiness of it all, happy families and everything. You only want to get back together because your tart is too young and financially demanding and your son won't have anything to do with you. I am not putting up with you for that, or frankly any other, reason. Now get the fuck out of my house before I throw you out, and never come back unless you want a knife between your ribs."

"No, no, no, you've misunderstood me. I've said it all wrong. Stella, I have realised that, despite everything, I need a real woman who understands me and knows how to look after me. Stella, I love you and want only you in my life. I said it wrong, please understand," was his weak and pathetic response.

"Listen, you spineless, self-absorbed, money-grabbing arsewipe, I am not interested in you, or anything you have to say. You can leave this house by your own means, or I can drag you out by your swollen testicles after I have again planted my foot between your legs for pleasure. Your choice, but you have five seconds to decide."

Tony took the hint and left the house quickly, tail between his legs and never to return, Stella hoped.

Once he had left, Stella refilled her glass and sat in the lounge, took a large swig and said to herself, "How dare he, what a bloody cheek, to think I would take him back simply because he has screwed it all up and wants to pretend it never happened. God, I am so lucky to be rid of that parasitic, self-absorbed man." She did feel sorry for him, the fact that his cock and arrogance had thrown away such a lengthy marriage and partnership, but she had moved on and was enjoying a new-found freedom of life which she didn't want to give up. At the end of the day, it was his problem, not hers, and he would have to deal with it without her. She smiled to herself, as she slowly calmed down, knowing she had made the right decision.

The rest of the day passed without event, and Stella spent the time relaxing and thinking about the last few months, the holiday, now oh-so near, the future and the different paths she may find herself treading. None of them worried her and she was truly looking forward to the next few years of continued re-awakening and growth. She was content, and that is precisely how she went to bed that night.

Chapter 20

Stella was getting ready for work when her mobile rang, it was David. "Hi David, I was just about to leave for work, all OK?"

"Yes, all fine," was the reply. "I was wondering if you wanted to pack a few things for a couple of days at mine? No pressure, but if you do, I'll call by and pick you up."

She knew he was keen but didn't realise quite how struck he must be on her. "Hell yes, give me fifteen minutes then," was the immediate response.

"Great, see you in fifteen."

Stella was excited again, a few more days with David, all thoughts of Lesley went out of the window as she hurriedly changed out of her cycling gear and had another panicked hunt through the wardrobes trying to find a few bits to go into an overnight bag. Once more she was off for some fun with her boss!

David arrived and seemed pleased to see her, and with the fact she had agreed to spend a few more days with him. They talked generally about the weekend while he drove the few minutes to the office. '*That hill was much easier in a car*' Stella thought to herself. David had not been up to much but did spend time in the police station as it seemed sensible, given he was at a loose end. Stella slightly embarrassed, simply confirmed she spent the weekend at home and with friends – she didn't go into the detail of that! She confirmed her holiday gear had arrived and how excited she was about her impending holiday. She also told him about yesterday's visit from Tony. David had a chuckle when she told him he was sent away with his tail between his legs.

Once at work, Stella busied herself with banking and billing. Her head was down and she was furiously checking and cross checking all the items to match the computer records to the paper ones. Things were looking good and David had set up an online account for the VAT. He was good at doing as he was told, she mused, perhaps a bit more dominance in the bedroom might be in order? She sat up and rubbed the inside of her thigh with a smile at the thought of later. She transferred the money due to the VAT man into the new account, and still the office account was looking good. David had popped out to court for a couple of regular clients, but would be back before lunch, he had promised.

Mid-morning, Stella had an email from the court, her divorce was progressing and the court had agreed her divorce issuing the actual date for the decree nisi and also agreeing that the financial settlement would be considered and hopefully approved on the same day as the decree absolute. The date for the nisi was set for the day before she went to Africa, what a celebration that would be.

David was indeed true to his word and brought in some lunch for them to share. It turned into a business meeting. They first discussed the new bank account. Stella confirmed she had access to it online and had already transferred the VAT money. The office account was looking good, and she had also prepared a cash flow for the next three months. It showed that the practice was doing nicely and was going to continue to expand. Stella told David now would be the time to look for the new solicitor with a view to them starting on the next rota or if necessary, the month before. David responded to Stella saying that was great, but before factoring that in, there was another matter that needed addressing. David told Stella that her performance over the last couple of months had been well beyond his hopes. She had sorted the finances out superbly, given him more time to increase income and turnover, and matters were now well settled. In addition, she had gone beyond her role with the business admin, was now costing and was more of an all-round office manager. The first thing he had to do was put her salary at a level commensurate with the work she was doing. There would be no argument and he was increasing her salary by £6000 per annum. Stella was gob-smacked by this, it was totally unexpected, but the practice could afford it. She jumped up from her chair and ran to him, thanking him with a hug and a kiss, that, had they not been in work would have developed to something much more serious, sensual and sexual!

At the end of the working day, which today was four p.m., David drove Stella back to his house. When she got there David handed her a gift.

"I was out in town waiting to go to the police station with a bit of time to kill. I saw this in a window and immediately thought of you, so I had to buy it. I hope you don't mind, and I hope you like it."

Stella was speechless once more, and very embarrassed. She slowly opened the gift. He had bought her a bangle. It was wide with various bits cut through in an abstract style and made of silver. Quite thick and definitely far too expensive.

"Oh my god, thank you. What the hell have I done to deserve this?" she asked.

"Easy, you agreed to stay over."

This man was getting brownie points with every second they were together. Stella put it straight on. It was wonderful on and fitted just as she wanted, not so loose that it fell half way down her hand. David got a very sensual, deep and long kiss for his efforts. David was becoming aroused but he decided it was best to save that until later! Instead, he poured the wine and sat Stella at the kitchen table while he prepared a Thai red chicken curry from scratch. They talked as he cooked. Stella once again casting her gaze to David to take in every moment and savour her time with him.

Stella wanted to ask him to divulge his sexual fantasy but was too scared to ask him as it might lead to him asking about hers, and she wasn't ready to announce her bi-sexuality to him, not yet. So, she kept the chat light. They discussed her upcoming holiday and the clothing she had bought, the new camera and the excitement she felt. David had never been on safari and was jealous in a nice way and wished he was going with her. He confessed that he would miss her while she was away, both personally and at work.

David was wanting to confess his full feelings for her, which had developed very quickly. He saw a full future together with Stella, and hoped that this early lustful relationship would develop into a permanent fixture.

After dinner they shared a bath and went straight to David's bed. Both were ready for a great night of sex. Stella decided she would test out her theory of David's submissive nature and without saying a word she pushed him gently onto his back, straddling him and pinning his wrists above his head with her hands. She kissed his forehead, his eyes, his nose, cheeks and chin. She ran her tongue down his neck and chest to his stomach. She bought her head back up to his chest and opened her mouth wide, taking in the whole of his nipple without touching it. She let the tip of her tongue tease his nipple until it was erect. David sighed with pleasure. Then she took it in her teeth and bit, gently but getting harder and harder. David arched his back in the excitement of the pain and audibly took a sharp intake of breath. Stella moved on to the other nipple and gave it the same treatment, still David's hands were firmly held above his head.

Stella moved down. His penis was erect already she saw, and the tip was moist, he was loving it. She lifted her head and said, "I'm going to release your arms now, but do not move them." There was no response, but she let them go. She spread his legs and knelt between them. Stroking his inner thigh with her hands, moving round to the underside of his testicles, then cupping them and rolling them in her hand, the other hand teasing the bottom of his penis before returning both hands to his inner thigh. She moved further down the bed and spread his legs wider before performing the same acts with her tongue, each time she found a spot he jerked in pleasure, his penis twitching with excitement and desire, but not yet. Slowly and carefully, she led her tongue from the bottom to the top and back down, taking her time, savouring his hardness. The juices from within him were now leading a path from his tip to his stomach and she took the moisture on her tongue. The simple act led to more escaping from him and she again took it inside her mouth.

After working him into this frenzy for a while, she decided that he had earned her mouth and she took him inside her, very slowly and carefully, down and down until she could feel him at the back of her throat. She held him there and used her tongue to massage him, feeling him twitch and jerk inside her mouth. She took her hand and cupped his testicles once more, then moved her middle finger further down and round between his cheeks, massaging the entrance of his bottom gently. His body was now physically jerking he was so aroused. Her finger entered him, and the finger and mouth worked in tandem to pleasure him until he exploded into her mouth.

She got up and came to lie beside him. He looked over and said, "Where the hell did that come from? That was incredible."

Stella chuckled and said, "You have a lot of catching up to do! Sex has moved on quite a lot in the last few years. I hope together we can develop. Don't get me wrong, you are awesome in bed and we are just getting to know each other, but we have lots I want to try with you. We can discuss it more another day. I just want to sleep in your arms now."

David kissed Stella on the cheek and she snuggled in to him and fell asleep. David remained awake for a while pondering what she meant, but happy in the fact that she saw this as at least a medium-term relationship. David thought about Stella, and how she had come to him quite by chance and how the relationship had developed. He was very happy, especially now they were lovers. He made the decision that he was not going to let her go, if he could avoid it.

Tuesday and Wednesday disappeared in a flood of paperwork, courts, bills and phone calls by day, followed by total contentment, relaxation, comfort and passion by night. It wasn't until Thursday that things changed.

David drove himself and Stella to work. He dropped her off and said he had to go to court, which Stella knew anyway. On her own now, Stella made a cup of tea and settled down in her office. Paperwork and the weekly bank reconciliation were her tasks for the day. She sent Brian an email to keep him in the loop regarding Tony and to confirm the dates the court gave her. At about eleven thirty the front door opened, which for a criminal firm was unusual, and Stella went to see who was in the office and if she could help. Standing in the reception area (for want of any other meaningful expression for the void with a few chairs,) was Lesley. She looked dreadful. As soon as she saw Stella she ran over to her, flung her arms around her and began to sob. Stella could see by the mascara-streaked cheeks this was not the first time today either. She held her tight and comforted Lesley for what appeared an age, but was in reality, only a few minutes before she felt that Lesley had calmed down enough to be able to speak.

"What on earth is going on? You've never been here before and now here you are sobbing. What's happened? Sit down in my office and I'll make some tea." She led Lesley to her office and sat her in a chair before going to the kitchen. When she returned, Lesley had her face buried in tissues trying to clear up the mascara and try and make herself look half presentable.

"Stella," she struggled to talk, "It's Sam. He rang this morning. He told me that he's had enough. He's found another job and his mother has convinced him that a fresh start all round is needed. He needs to be away from me and my spending. He says he's been thinking about it for a while and, well, we were drifting apart, but the latest spending of mine put the lid on the whole thing and talking it through with his mum, he's decided that the marriage is over, it's done. I think he has someone else lined up, but he wasn't saying. Oh my god Stella, I am so sorry. You're at work I know and we have been friends for only such a short time, but I feel really close to you, especially after last weekend and I didn't know who to turn to. You were the obvious choice. I am so sorry."

Bloody hell thought Stella, what a mess. Poor Lesley.

"Don't worry," she replied pointlessly, of course she would worry. "I'm sure things will work themselves out, as they always do. Anyway, look at me. A few months ago, I was where you are right now and now life couldn't be better. You will get through this. I'll be there and together, we will get this fixed."

Stella continued to comfort Lesley and they talked around the houses for about half an hour, then David returned to the office. Stella rushed out to meet him. "David, I am really sorry, but a friend of mine has turned up here. Her husband has just told her the marriage is over and she's in bits. She didn't know who else to turn to, so she came here. I am so sorry. I didn't know what to do and she's in my office really upset."

David took it all in his stride. "No problem, Stella. Why don't you take her home and take the afternoon off to see what can be done? It's a one off and I'm sure you're on top of everything as you usually are." He winked cheekily at her. "Just get her home safe and I'll see you here in the morning." Stella thanked David and took Lesley out of her office, introduced them to each other, which felt strange knowing that she was sleeping with them both and neither knew, before taking her to her car and getting her to drive to her own home. She took Lesley inside and poured two glasses of wine, they were needed by both of them.

"OK Lesley, let's start to work this out over a glass of wine. Sam. Tell me the detail about it all. I know you had a row about spending and he ran off to his mother. I know she doesn't like you, but this seems a bit drastic. What do you want to happen?"

Lesley looked at Stella, deep into her eyes, gripped the glass so tight Stella thought it might break and started, "When we first got together in the pub, and I kissed you in the car park, Sam saw. He had never seen me kiss a woman before and noticed that it was more than a peck. I told you I had seen other women before and Sam didn't know. That's all true. He quizzed me, but I didn't let on. He started going on about threesomes as the thought was really turning him on. I told him that it was all in his head. The night we came and stayed over he was pestering me to hit on you, which of course, I didn't in front of him. He knows nothing and never will. He fancies you and that made me worried for my marriage as I thought he might try for an affair with you."

"Well, he certainly hasn't, and I am not in the market," Stella interjected, shocked at the assertion.

"I know that. Please let me go on. We have argued about it, he seemed determined. Anyway, moving on. His job was on the line and money was getting tight. I was spending, but he can spend too, more than me most of the time. I don't know where it all goes and with me not working it was a problem, cards mounting up, you know the drill. We had a row and I think this has been the final straw. His mother has put her claws in, and the past few days have let him see a way out I suppose, in his head anyway. Now he wants to get on with his life and go on some sort of shag fest, if he hasn't already with his nights away. I think the marriage is done if I am honest. I will have to look for work again and that doesn't faze me, I may even start my own business. As for me, the last few weeks have brought us closer and closer, last weekend was beautiful, like a real couple. I've been with several women in the past, but no one has touched my heart and my mind like you have, Stella. You may not want to hear it, but I am falling in love with you. I'm ready to commit to you and to you alone. We are both bi-sexual and fuck knows how we're going to work through that, but I know I want to try. Me and you, as a proper couple. The Thurston dykes! I bet you didn't expect that."

"*Holy shit, no I didn't,*" was racing through Stella's head. "*What the hell do I say? This day was coming for sure, but not for months yet. There's David, heterosexual relationship in the making. I'm not ready to decide, to choose or to give either up. I need time to think this through, time to work out if I can have them both and maybe even others. I'm just out of one relationship and now I appear to have swapped it for two.*"

"Lesley, that is a bombshell I wasn't expecting. You're upset with Sam, and I'm not going to rush into a relationship with you, or anyone else at the moment. Christ this is all new to me, I'm finding my feet. Yes, we are great together, no better than that, we're natural together, it feels good without pressure. I don't want to charge into something new. Let's stay as we are for a bit, see how things pan out with Sam, he and you may change your minds. I'm here for you, that's for sure, but let's go at a walking pace not a sprint."

The reply was tinged with an element of sadness, "I know you're right Stella, a sensible and logical head, which I admire. It's true, it's early days for us and I accept entirely what you say about us and Sam. But at least it's out there and now you know how I feel. I'm here for you too, we'll continue to be great mates and have great sex together until you are ready to take it to the next level. I better get home I suppose and start to plan my future."

"No Lesley, you are not going home until the morning. Firstly, that's a big glass of wine you have emptied, and I am not letting you lose your licence. Second, we're mates and we're going to have a girly night in. We can talk about everything else you need to talk about and we can make some plans for you just in case Sam is serious. Now, tell me about this business idea of yours."

They spent the rest of the evening discussing Lesley's past before Sam, her family, education, work history, loves and her plans for the future. She surprised Stella when she told her she was a florist by trade and had great success doing weddings only. It was a company that had several contracts with the hotels, venues and planners in East Anglia, but she had given it up when Sam came along. They spent too much time together and weekends were too precious, got in the way of work. She could start that again quickly and the profit margins were immense. Stella agreed it was a great idea and she would use her business brain to get the paperwork side of things, business plans, letter head, website blurb etc. in hand.

Eventually, they went to bed together and once more did not have a sexual encounter, just a loving cuddle beneath the quilt and a sound sleep in each other's arms.

Chapter 21

Stella woke to find Lesley sound asleep next to her. She spent five minutes watching her sleep and breathe. It was a beautiful and mesmerising experience. She felt all of the pain Lesley was going through and truly wanted to help. She had feelings for Lesley, that much was clear, but was she ready to go public? More importantly, was she ready to tell David? She knew the answer deep down. Relationships are built on trust and honesty. If she kept this from David, then the whole relationship was a fraud. If she kept David from Lesley, the same thing applied. She didn't like dirty secrets and knew she must come clean about it, with both of them. Hopefully one, or both of them, would understand. If not, she would be spending more time in London with Julie she figured. Life was there for her to enjoy and she would enjoy it openly and honestly.

Stella went downstairs and took up some fruit juice for her and Lesley, who by now was starting to stir. They had a quick morning cuddle and decided they could share another five minutes together as Lesley would drop her at work. The time they spent together was precious to both of them. Stella left Lesley in bed and went for a shower first, then Lesley jumped straight in while Stella got herself dressed and put her face on. It wasn't long before Lesley was taking Stella on the short car ride to work. It was at this point Stella decided she must tell Lesley the truth.

"Lesley, we spoke yesterday about our feelings for each other and everything I said was true. There is, however, one small complication we need to think about. You're bi-sexual and so am I. That's great, as we understand each other. I need to be honest with you as it's important for any relationship, sexual or otherwise. I've started to see a man. You remember David, my boss, from yesterday? Well, we've been seeing each other and I think it has potential. I haven't told him about us yet and I intend to do that today so we all know where we stand. I have no idea what he'll say, but I do know he will need to accept me as bi-sexual for it to work. Quite how this works in practical terms I have no idea, but I don't intend to go sneaking around like you have with Sam."

Lesley slowed the car down while she thought for a moment. "Oh Stella, I know you like men as much as I do, and thank you for being so honest. I hope he does understand, he's quite hot to look at by the way. No matter what he says, and no matter what happens, I hope we at least have a friendship, even if it's platonic. As you say you, no, we all, need to work out the practicalities of your sex life." With that she laughed.

Stella felt relieved at her honesty and gave Lesley a kiss on the cheek as she got out of the car and went into work. She made a coffee and got straight down to catching up with the work she didn't get done yesterday afternoon. She had to make this up to David. David! She had to tell him and today. When would be best? At work? Over dinner? In the bath, god no – before that.

David arrived a short time later and Stella made him a coffee. She was nervous and was sure it showed. Stella didn't want to tell him, but knew she had to. How any coffee made it from the kitchen to David's desk will forever remain a mystery, her hand was shaking the whole way. He was due to be in the office all day doing casework, unless he got a call to go to the police station. He worked for about an hour and that gave Stella time to press on with her work, although it was proving difficult today. Uppermost in her mind was the fact that she knew she had to have a conversation with David, and she was worried about what his reaction might be. She didn't want to lose him as a lover, but she also didn't want a relationship with him built on a lie, especially a lie like hers – more so because it was hers.

David came into her office and sat down. "I need a break, that evidence I've been looking through for the last hour has sent my eyes all fuzzy and scrambled my brain a bit, so I thought I'd come and see my favourite office manager for ten minutes, if that's OK?" It was, of course, rhetorical, he was the boss and Stella was hardly likely to turn him away. He continued, "So what was the issue with your friend yesterday? I hope the two of you managed to work it through and she's OK now."

Stella saw the opportunity and decided that it was now or never. "Well David, that was Lesley, we met in The Fox a little while ago and became friends. She's married to Sam and, sadly, it seems their marriage is over, Sam wants a divorce. He's left and moved in with his mum. She didn't know who else to talk to. I hope you don't mind, and I've nearly caught up with the work I missed yesterday."

David laughed. "It's seriously not a problem, you work hard, I appreciate that and it's swings and roundabouts as far as I am concerned, so long as the work gets done, I'm fairly easy with it."

"Oh David, you're a really great boss, thank you, I appreciate it too. I need to have another conversation with you though, and I have no idea what to say or what you will say when I tell you, but I need to. It's a conversation I must have but it frightens me."

David looked both puzzled and concerned. "What's the

matter? Don't say you are leaving? Or are you getting cold feet about our personal relationship?"

Stella looked away from him, embarrassed. This was a conversation she had never ever expected to have in her whole life. "I'm not quitting, I love my job. I'm also not ending our personal relationship, although you might, but please hear me out. I had only ever been with Tony from university, faithful and a totally monogamous relationship as far as I was aware. I am not the sort to go chasing round for sex, never have and never will. When we split up, I was alone and socialised on my own in The Fox. There I met Lesley as you know, and we became friends. The other night, in bed, I told you that you have lots to learn about sex and so did I, in fact I still think that I have lots more to learn. I'm loving life at the moment, work, us, freedom. I'm also starting to feel really close to you and I don't want to lose you David, not for a moment, which is why I am taking forever to tell you what I need to. I want to be honest with you. I don't want to and won't have secrets, that is no basis for any relationship to work, and I want ours to work."

Stella lifted her head to look David straight in the eye. "Oh bugger it. Lesley and I, we're more than friends. We enjoy each other's company and we have sex with each other. Lesley was the first and she has opened my eyes and body to the fact that I am bi-sexual. I'm sleeping with you and I'm sleeping with her. Both of you are fantastic but in totally different ways. I really can't say much more, there it is, I've told you. Please god, don't tell me that's the end for us."

David sat, open mouthed at the revelation. This was all brand-new territory to him. "Jesus Christ," was the best expletive he could find for the situation at such short notice. "Wow! I don't know what to say. If you were ever going to give me bad news, then this would be the last thing I would ever have thought you would say. I need some time simply to get my head round this. Don't get me wrong when I say that though. You have some idea as to how I feel about you and that hasn't changed. This revelation is far, far from anything I was expecting. Never ever have I been in a relationship like this. What, how, why and where all need to be worked out. Stella, I understand now what you meant the other night and there was me feeling all inadequate by it. Just wow! OK, OK, nothing changes, you are still Stella, fantastic, sexy, loving, kind and all those things. I shouldn't be surprised, why should only men fancy you? You are still my Stella. Let me think about this and see how we can make this work. Any more revelations you want to floor me with? Bondage fetish, water sports, sex change, drugs? Best we deal with it all now."

Stella continued to look into David's eyes and saw confusion. "Water sports, not ever, never ever. No drugs or sex change, but bondage could be an interesting proposition, not that I have ever done that either. I understand the shock, I didn't think this would ever be me, but Tony has freed me, and I want you to continue with me on my journey, not just sexual revelations but a total discovery of who I really am. Most of it should be a good ride, but no doubt there will be things I don't like along the way, but I at least want to try. This safari trip, I'm nervous and excited but rest assured I will not be looking for a lover while I'm away. It's a trip for me to search for myself and develop my link with nature and the world. I understand you need time to let it sink in and I will give you that time, please think it all through. God David, I'm falling in love with you." Stella was done. She looked down at her desk and placed her head in her hands, waiting and wanting a hug.

David confirmed he would give it all serious thought and no doubt there would be another conversation, and another at a later time, but he also had no plans to give her up either. He left her office and returned to his own, sat down and threw his head back, looking at the ceiling hoping the answer was written up there.

Meanwhile, Stella had assumed a different pose. Her head was now nestled between her arms on the desk and her eyes were closed tight. She felt awful. She felt sadness. She didn't feel regret. This had to be said and now she had done it. She wished it was a conversation she never had to have but it was done. Did she regret being bi-sexual or the things she had done? Not one bit, it was who she was. She hoped David would understand, she was sure he would, and she hoped further that he would be able to deal with it and they could continue the relationship as it was. Long term it could be tricky, but many people in similar situations seem to work it out fine, so why shouldn't they? Stella had absolutely no idea how this would end.

It was after lunch when David returned to her office. He walked round to her side of the desk and pulled her up from her seat. He took her in his arms and gave her a tight hug. Stella let her head rest against his chest, his heartbeat was gentle and solid. He rested his own head on hers and whispered into her ear, "I love you, Stella Green and I thought you needed this. You have done a very brave thing this morning and I respect you all the more for it." He held her for a few more moments before he let her go. Without saying another word, he walked back out of her office and into his own.

What the hell does that mean, she thought. Is it a good sign or is it the start of a gentle let down? She truly didn't know, but she was glad he had done it regardless. An hour later her phone pinged, a text. It was from David, in the other room! What the hell? She opened it. It read:

"I am on the phone to the cps, but want to know if you are coming home with me tonight? Xx"

"Oh, thank you! Yes please xx"

Went winging its way back within seconds, and for the first time that day, Stella felt like the weight of her confession was lifting from her shoulders. Then she heard from Julie, another text: *"Hey stranger, not seen you for a while, fancy spending some time with me this weekend. Would love to see you before you jet off."*

She replied:

"Well as I fly next week, we better make it for the weekend, how does Saturday suit, pop round for the afternoon we can catch up."

Julie confirmed and that was another date in her diary.

At the end of the day, David drove Stella to his house, and they began the ritual of Stella sitting at the table with a glass of wine, while David cooked dinner.

"You must let me cook for you David, it's not fair that you always seem to do it. Perhaps you should come to mine and stay over?"

David replied, "That's a delightful idea, I've been waiting for an invitation. By the way, how are you getting to the airport next week? I can drive you down if you want. I'd like to see you off."

Something Stella hadn't thought of yet, a great idea. "Well, that's a plan then, you can stay at mine the night before, I will cook for you and I'll let you take me to the airport, thank you David."

The lovers ate dinner and chatted, but it wasn't the same, it was quieter, there was an elephant in the room. Both knew it was there in the corner standing quietly and looking at them, neither wanted to mention it. Stella knew what the problem was, it didn't take a rocket scientist to work it out, but she couldn't push David. Let him work through it in his own time. He was entitled to have time to get his head straight, it was one hell of a bombshell she had dropped. They cleared the dishes away together and the atmosphere did not improve, their actions were perfunctory without any touching or laughing.

Then David said, "Can we go to bed please?"

"Of course," said Stella and they both went to David's room. Two quick showers, not shared, and they got underneath the quilt. Stella instinctively snuggled under David's arm, placing her hand across his chest, and David pulled her close placing his free arm on her shoulder.

Without looking at her David spoke, "Stella, I need to apologise. I have been very quiet tonight and there's been an atmosphere. We both know why, and I have been rude letting it get to me. You are a guest and my lover, and I shouldn't behave in that manner. I'm sorry. This is something so new and I'm still coming to terms with it. There are so many questions I want to ask and also don't, if that makes any sense? But we cannot let it come between us and spoil what we have, we have been lucky finding each other. Don't answer me, but things I am thinking about are, will you leave me for Lesley? How will I cope with you spending time with her and away from me? Will I get jealous knowing you are having sex with someone else? How will I deal with it? These are some of the questions I need the answers to. I just need time to get my head around it all. Do you understand?"

Stella pulled him tighter and kissed his chest, "David I know what I've said, and I try to put myself in your shoes, wondering how I would cope, and like you, I don't know the answer either.

No need for you to apologise at all. Yes, tonight has been uncomfortable but we know why. I'm just grateful I'm here in your bed with you, rather than home alone having just screwed up a great relationship. Take as much time as you need. I am sure there must be stuff out there on the internet that might help. I don't know."

"I hadn't thought of that. Maybe at the weekend I can do some research and see what I can find out. I need to sort this out for both our sakes. In the meantime, please bear with me. Do you mind if we just go to sleep tonight?"

Stella moved from under him, looked him in the eye and said "Of course not David, it's been a difficult day for both of us. Goodnight." She kissed him on the lips and cuddled back down to go to sleep. David said goodnight, and switched the light off.

The next morning Stella woke to find David already gone. She went downstairs to hunt for him. She found him in his study in his dressing gown at his desk.

"Morning Stella, got up early and decided to grab the bull by the horns. You're right, loads of stuff out there, but it'll take a little time to get through. I'm feeling much more positive this morning."

The atmosphere was much warmer and Stella began to relax once more. She got ready for work and by the time her face was on David was ready to.

At the end of the day, which passed without incident, David sent her home early. "You must have loads to do to get ready for next week. Have a great weekend." He gave her a kiss and she once more, although the first time in a while, got on her bike and cycled home alone.

Chapter 22

Stella got home after work the next day, put her bike away and poured herself a big glass of wine. She needed it. She sat on the sofa in silence, looking blankly at the window into the street and clutching the glass of Chablis. Her thoughts were dominated by David and Lesley. What a mess she found herself in. Her brain was telling her to choose and stick with just David, that is what she had been brought up to believe was right. After all, she had been heterosexual her whole life except for the last few months. Her heart however, was torn in two. Lesley was kind, sensual, sexy, caring, and the two had enormous fun, but she didn't know if it would last and what about everyone else finding out? But why should she even care about what others thought? Conditioning, she thought. David was also kind, sensual, sexy and caring, but she didn't see him being as much fun, bit more staid, and a safer bet in daily life and long-term. It is also what would be expected of her. She would be left with a void; would she be happy and content living with the void? She didn't know. Maybe she wouldn't have to choose and David would be the one who made the ultimate choice.

She text Julie. Told her she was home for the weekend and would be available anytime. Julie replied, informing Stella that she was at a loose end herself tonight so would come over if that was OK. Stella was delighted with that and told her to get straight over. Her company would be good tonight, she needed someone to talk it through with.

It wasn't long before the familiar sight of Julie's car pulled up on the drive. The door was opened and Stella greeted her with a tight hug and Julie responded in kind. The pair went into the lounge and Stella poured some wine into the glass that she had already got out for her arrival. They sat on the sofa at either end as they always did with their legs entwined in the middle.

Julie spoke first, "I was going to talk about your holiday next week and get all jealous of your adventure, but by the look on your face there are more important things to discuss. What's up honey?"

That was enough. Stella started to cry. "I think I've screwed up Julie. I may have lost David. I wanted to be honest with him. I told him about Lesley and my bi-sexuality. I don't know if he understands or if he can deal with it. It might be the end for us. I spent last night with him and there was a huge atmosphere, it was not pleasant. He did say he didn't want it to end between us and needed time to get it into his head, but I'm not so sure."

Julie stood up and put her glass on the table. She took Stella's glass and placed it beside hers, she made Stella sit up. She climbed behind her on the sofa, spread her legs so Stella was nestled between them and pulled her in tight. Julie wrapped her in her arms and stroked her hair. She felt her stomach ache, like it did when she was with Amy. "My poor Stella," she said. "Don't worry, it'll all be just fine. David will see it for what it is, and if he truly wants you then you'll work something out that suits you both, or should I say, all. Did I tell you I'm still in touch with Amy? She wants to see me again. I'm finding it exciting and confusing."

"No, you didn't let that one out." Stella sat up and grabbed the glasses, passing Julie hers and remained nestled between her legs. Julie told her that they had been texting each other, and Amy had such fun that she wanted them both to come back down to London for a weekend again. Stella said why not get her to come up here? They could stay at hers and it would be a great girlie weekend. That was a plan set for the future. Stella had her hand on Julie's thigh and Julie was still stroking Stella's hair. Now Stella was feeling tingly.

Stella got up, she wasn't ready to spoil the friendship and instead went to get a bottle to top up the glasses. Asking if Julie was staying first, before refilling Julie's glass. They ordered a Chinese to be delivered and settled in for an evening together. The pair discussed Julie's life, her husband and her children. It was a good marriage, but now she too had a secret and this secret was not about to be told. They discussed Tony and the settlement offered to Stella. The conversation Stella had before throwing him out, and then they got back to Lesley and David. There were no solutions found but at least Stella was able to talk about it without dissolving into tears.

It was getting late and the tipsy pair decided it was bed time. For the first time, and for no real reason, Stella took Julie to her room. They both undressed down to their underwear and climbed under the duvet. Stella put the TV on and Julie snuggled under Stella's arm. They stayed cuddled together and the next thing Stella knew was Julie, fast asleep in her arms. She gently rolled her over, turned the TV off and pulled the duvet up before closing her eyes and falling asleep herself.

The next morning, they both spent time in the shower and then shared the breakfast duties. Stella felt alive again. No matter what David decided, Stella would not be able to give up the feelings and needs she had for the feminine form. They discussed the holiday over breakfast, and Julie was indeed jealous of her plans. They decided that trying to get Amy up to Suffolk for the weekend would be a great idea, and Stella's house provided good cover for Julie. Stella hoped Lesley would come to make a four for the evening. Both agreed that would be a great idea and something to sort out when Stella got back from her holiday. Julie left Stella with a huge hug and a kiss wishing her well and hoping to see her soon.

The night with Julie had helped Stella get things into perspective. This was her life and it would be played out her way. Sure, she would make mistakes along the way, that was human nature, but also, she would not make sacrifices she didn't want to make. That was how it was going to be, and David would accept it or, simply, he wasn't the man for her. She loved him, but she loved herself and her life more. She wanted to be happy without compromise. Hopefully, she thought, that wasn't too selfish of her.

Saturday continued with a long chat with Brian. They wouldn't be in touch for about a month now, and she would miss him dreadfully, but it would all be good when she got back. Once she had decided her path in life, she would have to tell him, but he would understand. He was a different generation, more tolerant, more understanding. As for him, life was good, and the girlfriend was proving an added bonus. They would definitely come and stay for a weekend when she got back, this she looked forward to immensely.

Several hours passed with Stella tidying up the house, a final Hinch before her holiday. The packing began, but before she could do that, she decided she needed to reduce the amount of things she had put out for the holiday. Did she really need four swimsuits? She had a generous baggage allowance, but would be carrying it all every day on safari, so she only needed to take enough to see her through. There would be laundry facilities and given how it works, the various camps must have it off to a fine art. Four days maximum of clothing was the final decision, and so the task of selecting items from the nine days' worth on the bed began. The thinning out process was tedious and not fun, so Stella was relieved when the doorbell rang.

She walked downstairs she recognised the outline through the frosted window. It was Tony. What now? She thought he had got the message last time. As the door opened, she saw the state of him. He looked awful. When had he last slept and who is it that wasn't ironing his clothes? Once more, she felt a tinge of sadness for the man. The man who she had spent more of her life with than any other human being on the planet. It was hard, but then again, whose fault was it? How long would it take her to get him totally out of her system? The mind was steadfast, he was cheating scum who also wanted to cheat her out of her entitlements on divorce, had she not been so smart. But her heart remembered the university undergrad who swept her off her feet and with whom she had many happy years, with whom she produced a son. "Come in," was all she could say. "You better go through to the kitchen, I don't want you staining the sofa, you look bloody awful, and grubby too."

He walked through to the kitchen in silence, gone was his arrogance, and that confident streak he always had was missing, presumably left in a clean suit hanging in some wardrobe somewhere. Tony sat on a bar stool and held his head in his hands. "Stella, I don't know what to do or who to turn to. It's a disaster and now there's no way out. I know you told me never to come back, and I'm sorry, but you're the only one who I can talk to. It's Sue. I told you we weren't getting on. My mother hates her, thinks she's only with me for money. Now she's decided she's pregnant." Tony looked up and directly at Stella,

"Pregnant! Christ, I don't want any more children, not at my age, I want Brian, not another one. We discussed it, well when I say discussed, more a heated argument, I told her that she would have to have an abortion, I was told old to have a baby in my life. She said no. I shouted at her, 'you will get rid of it', poor choice of words I know. 'It, it!' she screamed back at me 'it's our baby, our child, not an it and I will not get rid of the baby, for you or anyone else.'"

Tony's head once more returned to look down at the kitchen worktop. "The argument got worse and worse and well, I hit her, just a slap, but a hard one, around the face, left a mark too, probably a black eye. She went for me and I ran out of the house. Left my phone. I spent the night in the car. I couldn't go to mums; she would go ballistic at me too. Christ Stella, I have never hit a woman. Even when you found out about Sue the row was nowhere near as bad as this. I don't know what to do. If I go home, what will I be facing? A girlfriend with a black eye, a policeman? Help me Stella, please."

Stella took another look at him and the pity left her. The heart was healing now he was a domestic abuser and his selfishness would let him deal with the consequences of his actions – Sue's pregnancy and his child. "Tony, I have no idea why you came here. I have no idea why you thought I would help or indeed how you thought I could help. You've taken your arrogance to new heights and now you admit to hitting a woman because she is carrying your child, conceived by your lust without thinking about the consequences and she refuses to have an abortion? You really have sunk to an all-time low in my eyes. I am trying desperately to move on with my life and once more you have chosen to interrupt it with your own problems, not my problems, in the hope that I'll fix them for you and make it all better. That,

Tony, is never going to happen. Not today, next week or ever. You deserve to have a policeman waiting for you when you get home, and an injunction to keep you away. Just don't call David Hughes. He can't help you since I work there, and he's my boyfriend. Now, can you please take your pity and get out of this house, and for the last time, never ever come back."

Tony could tell from the tone in Stella's words that this was the end of the conversation and any hope of a reconciliation. He got up from the stool and as quietly as he entered, he left. This time he would never return.

Once again it was turning out to be a stressful day and Stella needed to sit down with a glass of wine to let this latest intrusion into her life get processed in her head. How could he think for even a millisecond that his behaviour would get any sympathy from her, let alone advice or comfort? What an idiot. The part of her heart that still held some feeling for him had closed itself completely, and she was relieved. No more would he be a feature in her mind that would disturb her any more than a stranger at the door selling dishcloths.

After some processing, a text to Lesley asking to meet her before she went away was gratefully accepted by Lesley. She said she would come round tomorrow and did Stella fancy a mooch around Norwich? If so, she would pick her up at ten. Stella thought it was a great idea and readily agreed to it. Now she had to get back upstairs and continue the arduous task of sorting through her safari packing to make it as light as possible. That continued to be a struggle, but in the end, she decided that going native was the only way. No makeup, except lipstick and one bottle of perfume, no hairdryer, and further limiting of clothing required. Eventually, the task was complete and she managed to be able to carry the bag on her shoulder with her camera gear in another bag. That would have to do. A quick, light dinner and bed was required. Too tired for a bath so she took a quick shower instead.

The next morning Stella was excited at the prospect of another day out with Lesley. Stella got out of bed and pulled back curtains to witness the dawning of a beautiful day. The red tinged sky as the sun crept up, birds flying, rushing anywhere and everywhere. Today was going to be a good day, she decided. She hadn't been to Norwich in forever and was looking forward also to spending time with Lesley. On the dot she arrived and after a hug and a kiss the pair set off. The drive along the A11 was tedious but thankfully only half an hour or so and chatting with her girlfriend made the journey far better. They parked in tower ramparts and were soon walking along in the city centre. She had forgotten how pretty parts of it were, the old architecture and independent shops that still managed to survive somehow. It was sad to see that there were also the multi-nationals taking up much of the prime space in an attempt to turn the shopping area into the same as any other, but that was how it was. At least Norwich wasn't boarded up like so many dying high streets. They walked through the Chapel fields Centre and window shopped some clothes. Lesley was counting pennies as Sam had still not returned, and Stella was too busy thinking about her holiday to concentrate on clothes. But, hand-in-hand, it was a pleasurable experience. They found themselves in The Maid's Head for a spot of lunch. It was a nice hotel with a lovely comfortable and private lounge where they could talk more easily. The hotel was a bit pricey and the food had gone downhill, but it was not a chain, which they both despised.

While they were waiting for the food to arrive, Lesley started updating her about Sam. He had come clean about the new girlfriend and now divorce was on the cards. At least his job now seemed safe and they were talking civilly to each other. Lesley confirmed that she still needed Stella's help in setting up her new business, but that could wait until she was back from her holiday. She was looking forward to this new challenge, as was Stella in helping her friend out.

It was then Lesley chose to ask about David. She was being selfish, she didn't want to lose Stella, but understood. Although judging by today, Stella wasn't going anywhere to soon. "So, did you tell David? How did he take it? Where does it leave us?"

Stella gave an honest and open reply to the questions, explaining that David had taken it as she would have taken it herself. He was still reeling and trying to work it out in his head, but he wanted to be with her. She would give him time to work it through, of course, but at the end of the day, she was not ready to give Lesley up. Lesley was relieved.

After lunch they returned to the car and Lesley drove Stella home. Stella invited her in, she needed to feel her naked skin against hers. She sent Lesley to get the bed warm while she fetched two glasses and the bottle, and then she took them upstairs. Lesley was ready for her and Stella stripped and climbed in beside her. They cuddled each other lovingly and chatted more while drinking their wine. They made late afternoon love and at the end, both were falling deeper into the relationship than they ever felt they would. There was no way Stella could ever give up Lesley, and that was now a fact.

Chapter 23

Lesley stayed for the rest of the evening and slept with Stella once more. Apart from getting another bottle of wine and some junk food to nibble on, the duo never left the bed. They made love to each other the next morning, a parting gift of each other's desire, before Stella went away. Both would miss each other in what would be a long three weeks apart. They went their separate ways, and each had a tear in their eye as they hugged by Lesley's car, Stella astride her bike to go to work. It was a long ride to work and Stella had her mind on the future with Lesley and how David was going to feel. He would be the one in her bed that night before the trip to the airport tomorrow.

When she arrived at work, she was shocked to find David had managed to get there first. She normally beat him to the office, when they came separately, these days. She walked in to find the coffee had already been made and gifts were also on her desk. David had bought her a journal so she could keep a diary of her adventure, and also a Swahili phrase book. Stella picked them up and flicked through each. She smelled each of them, both fresh and new, the leather on the journal especially fragrant, it made her feel warm. It was incredibly thoughtful of him, and Stella saw this as a good sign. Stella immediately walked into his office to thank him, he stood and the pair enjoyed a warm and tight embrace, Stella as a thank you and David as a good morning I missed you.

Stella had much to do to get the office in shape for her

planned absence. The day was spent getting the banking right up to date, getting other bills ready and using the online facility to set up payments due to go out while she was away. David kept trying to interrupt and have general conversation, but Stella kept throwing him out of the office. Conversation could wait until they were at home, her home.

David felt aggrieved by her rejections, although he understood how dedicated she was to her work and her desire to make sure everything, as far as possible, was done. This one of her many talents and something he truly appreciated.

It was a long day and by the time Stella had finished everything she had to do, including making sure her desk was tidy and leaving a list of financial matters for David to keep an eye on while she was away, it was after four p.m. David was itching to get away and spend the evening relaxing at Stella's. This would be a first for them both and he couldn't wait. "Enough, Stella," he said with some dominance. "The rest can wait until you get back. I want you to myself without any distractions. I've been waiting all day for some personal time with you."

"You're making an assumption there," was the reply but with a cheeky grin. "Okay, let's go. I'm going to make you a soufflé for supper and it needs looking after so you'll have to share me with the cooker."

David put Stella's bike into the back of his car and drove her home. This was odd indeed, for Stella she had never had a man stay over in her bed, not since Tony left. Trying to hide her nerves, she opened the door and invited David in. "I suppose I better show you around," and with that gave David a brief guided tour of her home.

David was surprised at how different it was compared to his, it was much brighter, lighter and very modern. The oversized bath in the en-suite was also very inviting and he secretly hoped they would share that later.

Back downstairs, she sat David at the breakfast bar and poured him a glass of chablis, perfect for the soufflé, then she got straight down to making the dinner. The chat was light and the atmosphere pleasant. David kept getting up from his seat and coming round to the business end of the kitchen to hug Stella from behind and kiss the back of her neck. For his trouble he was swotted several times with a tea towel, but it was all in good humour and Stella was relishing the attention, even if it did distract her from the tricky task of a perfect soufflé. She popped it into the oven and prepared the veg for steaming. Stella topped David's glass up, she gave him a kiss and said, "There I can relax a bit more now that's in the oven, but I still need to keep an eye on it. You can set the table. Have a cupboard hunt for what you need. It'll keep you out of mischief for a while!"

David laughed and began his search for cutlery, crockery, place mats and napkins. All were quickly located as they were in places where David, himself, might had put them. He set the table and returned to his wine.

It wasn't long before dinner was ready and on the table. "I will miss you, Stella Green, I mean I will really miss you. The past few months have been a real rebirth for me, at work and at home. I am enjoying my life for the first time in years and I want it to continue. Having said that, I also want you to go away and forget about everything and have a wonderful time. It's been tough for you and you need a break from reality, although I think you have coped wonderfully."

"Oh David, thank you, and thank you again for the parting gifts. We are a good couple with potential to make a great team.

I love my work and want to develop the firm with you over the next few years and I also want to make our relationship stronger and fuller and even more exciting. There are many more experiences I want for us, socially, together getting stronger."

David smiled and the conversation of mutual appreciation continued. Talk moved on to the holiday, what to expect and how wonderful it would be. Too soon the meal was concluded, to David's satisfaction. The soufflé had turned out well and not collapsed, much to Stella's relief. Stella and David, as was their habit at his house, cleared away the dishes and Stella said she would run a bath for them both to enjoy.

With the bath run, Stella led David upstairs once more and together the climbed in through the mass of bubbles. David was visibly relaxing and as their naked legs touched under the water, there was a sense of belonging that came over him. Stella's breasts were barely covered and her head tilted back as she allowed the feeling of unwinding to wash over her whole self.

David lay but never for one second took his eyes from her. He was relishing every moment of being here, with her. Stella had turned some light music on in the background and they lay in silence and contentment for what seemed like an age. There was the odd sentence from one or other, but nothing much. This was a moment of tranquillity to savour. They both did that beautifully. Stella thought back to the time she was alone in the bath dreaming of David. She smiled to herself in the satisfaction that her fantasy had turned into a reality.

Totally relaxed and with the water beginning to chill, it was time to get warm again. They left the safety of the disappearing bubbles and quickly towelled before jumping under the duvet and snuggling together, each seeking out the others body for warmth. This was going to be a night where they would make love to each other several times. Initially it was warm and gentle, but later it was more urgent, more demanding, more passionate and then, simply just because they could. They made love until it was well past the witching hour when they fell asleep.

Stella woke early the next morning, the excitement of her trip blasting her into consciousness. It was too early, but she couldn't go back to sleep. David lay beside her, breathing steadily, the duvet pulled round him tight, just his head visible. She watched him and smiled to herself. Then she remembered her problem, no, David's problem. It was unresolved, and David had not mentioned it at all. Was it to return and remain the elephant in the room? They couldn't continue like that, secret meetings with Lesley would ruin the relationship with David. It all had to be above board, in the open, if it was ever going to work at all. Even though she had a wonderful night with David, loved his company and had fallen for him, she could still not contemplate giving up Lesley, she craved the excitement she brought with her, the naughtiness, the wonderful new fulfilment that was so different from being in a heterosexual relationship.

She carefully left the bed and went downstairs to make herself a coffee. Her robe was loosely tied as usual and she sat at the breakfast bar holding the cup between both hands. Raising her head to the ceiling she sighed. It was a two-fold sigh. The first element was the contentment she felt right now, with David upstairs and the second element was the problem and the potential loss of him for Lesley. Both thoughts were still running through her head when David wandered in. He gave her a hug and she made him a coffee.

"Penny for them?" he said, as he kissed her forehead good morning.

"Oh David, you know what it is I am thinking about. You

know how I feel being with you. Having you here for the first time last night was, for me, the next step in our relationship. We're moving forward, yet standing still. I still don't know what your feelings are about Lesley, if you can cope with it, how we can work through it, if we can work through it?"

"Well, as I said this is new to me. I don't want to lose you. You know I've been doing research around the topic and trying to understand. There is so much information out there. Stuff on the emotional side, lots on transgender issues, and stuff on the physical side. You said to me once that I have a lot to learn, and I really believe that I do. Sexually, I'm not as experienced as I think you are and it seems we have a number of things that we should think about. There are clubs for swapping partners for example, out of my league I would be far too embarrassed. There are gay clubs, bi-sexual clubs, you name it and it's out there."

He sat on a stool and faced her. "I wasn't naive enough not to be aware of it because of the work I do, but really, the research I've done has been a real eye opener, I can tell you. Whatever happens this will have to be a gradual suck it and see, excuse the pun. I've even thought that perhaps the way forward would be for a threesome." His eyes flicked around the room. "You know, me, you and Lesley. I don't know how you feel about that, me with you both. I don't know how I would feel either and she needs to be happy too. At least that way it's out there, in private/public, not like cheating. I'm rambling now, sorry."

He returned his gaze to Stella. "At the end of it all, it seems there are a number of things we can do. Perhaps we can introduce Lesley into our relationship as a friend, so I get to know her socially and see how that goes? Then the two of you could have your sex, and I might feel better if I at least know who you're with. It may feel different than it would if you were sleeping with another man. I'm rambling again. Let's use your holiday as a time to process this in all our heads and see if we can resolve it between us all when you get back. How does that sound?"

Had he really just said that? Why did she not think of that? Would it work? How would she feel? "David, you have been doing your research and thinking it through. I hadn't considered a threesome. Wow, now I have to think. Go jump in the shower, we need to get ready. This holiday will give us both thinking time."

Stella jumped in the shower once David had finished. The water and the soap washing over her and her head deep in thought of the latest option or solution to the problem. She wished Lesley was there, with her and David, and they were talking it through and then having a try. Six months ago, such a thought would have been seriously alien to her, but now it was a realistic answer.

They both got ready and left the house. Stella double checked everything, and David followed behind for a treble check. The house was secure. Stella's bag went in the boot and just before she got in the car, she checked the road. No Lesley. Oh, how she wanted her there for a last goodbye hug.

The drive to Heathrow was slow. Rush hour traffic combined with the M11 and the M25 – it was never going to be a breeze. David spent much of his concentration on the roads, but they did talk. The conversation was about the holiday, work, politics and the weather. They sang to the radio. They commented on the poor driving of others. They didn't talk about the new proposals. David parked in the short stay and insisted on making sure Stella got her bag checked in and got to the security gate. He could go no further and had to leave her there. They both had a tear in their eye as they gave one final hug and kiss before Stella was on her own. It was tight, loving and needed by them both. Just before

Stella went out of the view of non-travellers, she took a final look behind her. She saw that David was still there, watching her leave. Then, in the blink of an eye they could see each other no more.

Stella was on her own now and for the next three weeks. She passed through the body scanner and bag x-ray without incident. It was two hours before her flight and hunger, or nervousness, was making her stomach rumble. She tried to find a restaurant with a spare seat but this was difficult, eventually she managed, and ordered herself a breakfast and a glass of champagne. Champagne to start this holiday adventure was a great idea, she would make that compulsory for every future trip. The bubbles fizzed in her nose and she giggled to herself. Having eaten and calmed her rumbling stomach, she went on a tour of duty-free, finding herself in the book shop, she chose a crime novel to keep her occupied in the evenings and on the beach. She thought it apt, given her new career.

It was time to go to the departure gate. The gate was a long walk and as she went, she was looking at the other passengers also heading to their gates, where are they going? What are their lives like? It became a game to pass the time as she walked. Another security check and she was allowed into the gate holding area. She found a seat and waited, watching all the others who she was going to share the plane with to Nairobi. African families going home, couples and families, young and old. This was going to be a full flight.

Her thoughts turned to David and Lesley and the last few months. Stella was feeling positive for the future. The last few months had been a rollercoaster ride from the depth of despair, up and back down, round and round spiralling excitement through her veins. There had been tears and magnificent joy.

Looking back at how she was before she discovered Tony's affair and looking at herself now, the two were barely recognisable as the same person. It was amazing how much she had changed and how much further she thought she still had to go.

Her thoughts were disturbed by an announcement. "Ladies and gentleman, we're are now going to start boarding. First and business class passengers, please make your way to the left and premium economy to the right." The scrum to get onto the plane had started in earnest. Dutifully, she went right and fought her way past standard economy passengers blocking the right and wanting to board also. The lady smiled at her as she checked her ticket and scanned her passport before letting her move to join the queue to board. Stella smiled back and noticed the touching fingers as her passport was returned to her. This touch would have washed over her in her previous life, but now each look and each touch held far more, an unspoken meaning the answer known only to the giver and recipient. Stella found her seat and buckled up, looking out of the window at the other planes all waiting. This holiday would be a time for rest, a time for peace, a time for adventure and a time for thinking.

End